THE
ADVENTURES
OF
FAR NORTH
JOHNNY

JOHN HAUTAMAKI

PublishAmerica
Baltimore

Hardcover 9781629073484
Softcover 9781630048211
PUBLISHED BY PUBLISHAMERICA, LLLP
www.publishamerica.com
Baltimore

Printed in the United States of America

Contents

DEDICATION

I dedicate this book to Judy Drouét,
through whose amazing effort made this book possible.

FOREWORD

Born in a small, rural town, in the rugged Upper Peninsula of Michigan, Johnny, a teenage boy, lived a very adventurous life. Raised on a farm that backed up to an untamed national forest, Johnny spent a lot of time exploring in the outdoors. His dog, Butch, was included in many outings, along with Johnny's best friend, Sam. There was never a dull moment for Johnny. Being stuck in quicksand in rising water and hunting for a lost Indian cave of gold were a couple of Johnny's adventures. Johnny witnessed the power of a tornado that came through the farm. Fishing on a lake, Johnny and Sam were attacked by a monster fish. Johnny explored a mysterious swamp with its scary creatures. He and his friends were caught by Indians who worshipped rattlesnakes. Johnny fell in love with a neighbor girl during the haymaking season. Johnny and Sam had to climb a tree to get away from a bull moose and then were surrounded by a pack of wolves. During an outing with Butch, they were attacked by a mountain lion. As a contestant in a cross country ski race, Johnny was pursued by a pack of hungry wolves, forcing him to fly off a high cliff, on his skis. One of Johnny's and Sam's best adventures was searching for a sunken treasure of silver and gold coins.

CHAPTER 1
QUICKSAND

Johnny was a teenage boy who lived on a farm with his parents, two brothers, and two sisters, in Michigan's Upper Peninsula. Johnny worked hard on the farm doing chores, as well as helping with his father's logging business.

Sam was also a farm boy who lived about a mile from Johnny's farm. Sam's parents had a dairy farm, so Sam had to milk cows twice a day, seven days a week. Johnny and Sam had become best friends while working together during the summer and fall seasons, on each other's farms. During the summer, neighbors helped each other make hay. In the fall, they helped each other harvest oats and wheat.

It had been a morning that had started with a light rain which was perfect for fishing. After catching their limit of fish, the boys decided to head for home. Since they were already wet, the boys started walking through the river to get to the other side. The boys had used a large, fallen pine tree to cross the river earlier. Just before reaching the other river bank is when Johnny stepped in the quicksand.

"Help," yelled Johnny! "I just stepped in quicksand!" "Sam, hurry and get something to pull me out!" Sam found a long, dry branch from an old pine tree and handed one end to Johnny. "Hold on tight and I'll pull you out," said Sam. Johnny wrapped his hands around the limb and said, "Okay, Sam, pull hard." Sam dug his boot heels into the dirt on the river bank and pulled with all his might. After several tries, Sam said, "Johnny, I can't pull you out by myself; I'll have to go for help!" "Don't worry, Johnny, said Sam, I'll hurry back as fast as I can." "You hang in there, buddy, I'll be back soon," hollered Sam.

The water in the river was waist deep, but Johnny had sunken down into the quicksand and the water was now up to his chest. As Sam was leaving, Johnny yelled, "You'd better hurry; the water will start rising with this rain." With a serious, worried look on his face, Sam said, "I'll be back as soon as possible, Johnny." The rain was coming down harder and Johnny was having a difficult time standing up against the swift river current. The river was being fed by many small streams and would start rising fast.

With the water just below his armpits, Johnny tried pulling his feet out; this caused Johnny to lose his balance and his head went under the water. Thinking he was going to drown, Johnny used swimming strokes to get his head back above the surface. The rain was now coming down so hard, Johnny couldn't see. The icy cold rain, mixed with hale, stung Johnny's face, as it pelted him. I don't want to die so young, thought Johnny. The water was now up to the top of his shoulders. The current, once again, pushed Johnny's head under the water. Again, Johnny used swimming strokes to get his head back above the water. The river continued to rise and now was just under Johnny's chin. He couldn't hold on much longer and cried out in desperation, "HELP!" "Somebody help me!" The river current then pushed Johnny under the water again. This time, Johnny didn't have the strength to get back above the water. He knew he was going to drown, but would hold his breath as long as possible. Thoughts flashed through his mind; he was sad thinking he would never see his parents, brothers and sisters, friends, or his beloved dog, Butch again. Unable to hold his breath any longer, Johnny let the air out of his mouth and prepared to drown.

Just as the last bit of air passed his lips, Johnny felt a hand under his head. With his head being lifted out of the water, Johnny gasped for air. "I knew you would get back in time, Sam," gasped Johnny. Sam didn't answer and Johnny felt a strap slip around him and under his armpits. Through the blinding rain, Johnny looked up and saw a giant of a man looming above him. He had a black, bushy beard and was wearing buckskin clothes. The huge man dug his boots into the river bottom, pulling Johnny out of the quicksand and up onto the river bank. Exhausted, Johnny rolled over on his back looking for the giant man. He wanted to thank him for saving his life, but the man had vanished.

The rain had almost stopped when Sam and his father arrived with a rope. Sam hollered, "We're back, Johnny!" He felt sick in the pit of his stomach when there was no sign of Johnny in the river. Sam's father said, "He must have drowned and is under the water." Sam thought he was seeing a ghost when Johnny stood up in the tall grass and said, "I'm okay, Sam." A big grin came over Sam's face when he realized his best friend, Johnny was alive.

Sam asked, "How did you get out?" Johnny related the story about the giant man with a bushy black beard and how he was dressed. Sam's father said that he didn't know of anyone in this area who fitted that description. Sam's father said he had to get back to the farm to finish his chores. In his backpack, Sam had some fried egg sandwiches, homemade chocolate chip cookies, and a thermos of hot coffee. The boys decided to sit on the river bank and enjoy their lunch. The stringer of trout they had caught earlier was still attached to a small bush near the river's edge.

Brush was cracking behind the large, uprooted pine tree that had fallen across the river. Johnny said, "It's just some deer coming to the river for a drink." Much to the boys' surprise, an enormous black bear was crawling over the roots of the pine tree. "He must have smelled our fish," shouted Johnny. "Let's get out of here," yelled Sam. The boys took off running up the hill, leaving everything behind. The bear began chasing them rather than stopping to eat the fish. The boys were in good physical condition and could run fast; however, the bear was closing the distance between them.

At the top of the hill was a hay field and across the field was a farm where Johnny's Uncle Seth lived. By the time the boys got to the top of the hill, the growling bear had almost caught up with them. The boys couldn't make it across the field before the bear would catch them. There were two men and a dog near a pickup truck in the driveway. Johnny and Sam started yelling, "Help!" The men looked in the boys' direction and saw the bear chasing them. The dog raced across the field barking at the bear. The bear had caught Sam and knocked him to the ground. Sam pulled his knees up to his stomach and clasped his hands behind his neck. He could smell and feel the bear's hot, foul breath near his face, as the bear pinned him to the ground with his front paws. Sam closed his eyes and clenched his teeth waiting for the bear's long, yellow teeth to sink into his skull. The bear stood up on his hind legs, opened his mouth wide, moved his head from side-to-side and roared at the barking dog.

To Johnny's surprise, it was his own dog, Butch, who had come with his father to visit his uncle. Butch sensed that the boys were in serious trouble with the bear. He darted in and out, nipping at the bear, to distract him so the boys could get away. The bear was furious, growling and swinging its paws at Butch. Then it happened, one swipe caught Butch in his side, sending him through the air yelping in pain. Butch landed with a heavy thud and lay lifeless on the ground. Sam got up and was running behind Johnny, but the bear caught him and knocked him down again. This time the bear sunk his teeth into Sam's shoulder and Sam screamed from the pain. Johnny ran back toward the bear with his hunting knife in his hand. Johnny was hollering as he leaped toward the bear, aiming his knife at the bear's head. The bear let go of Sam, stood up and swung a paw at Johnny knocking him to the ground. Then the bear went after Johnny who was on his back. Johnny was kicking and hollering at the bear when it grabbed one of Johnny's legs in its mouth. Johnny felt the bear's long teeth sink into his flesh. The pain was so bad that Johnny almost passed out.

A rifle shot rang through the air and the bear dropped Johnny. It was Johnny's Uncle Seth that had fired the shot at the bear, grazing him on the back. The bear stood up on his hind legs, spun around, roared and headed back toward the woods. Johnny's uncle always kept a rifle, on a gun rack, in his pickup just in case he ever needed it. He was able to get it out and take a clear shot at the bear. With Butch lying motionless on the grass, Sam with a bear bite on the shoulder, Johnny bleeding from the bear bite on his leg and almost drowning after stepping in the quicksand, this had not been a good fishing trip.

Johnny's father and uncle raced out to the field in the pickup. They picked up Sam and Johnny and laid them in the bed of the pickup. They ripped their shirts into strips to wrap around the boys' wounds to stop the bleeding. Then they went over to Butch and bandaged his wounds. Butch was placed in the pickup bed along with the boys. The vet's place was on the way to the hospital, so Butch was dropped off there. Johnny's father told the vet to try and save Butch and left to get the boys to the hospital.

Johnny's Uncle Seth pulled into the emergency entrance at the hospital. Johnny's father went into the hospital and explained about the bear attack. Attendants with two stretchers on wheels came out and placed the boys on them. The doctor checked the boys to see if an artery had been punctured, but none had. The doctor said, "You boys were lucky to just have puncture wounds and no broken bones. If an artery had been punctured, you could have bled to death." The doctor cleaned their wounds and put in a few stitches. He gave the boys a shot to ward off any infection. He gave each boy some pills to take for the pain and an antibiotic medicine for infection. Sam's left arm was put in a sling and attached to his body. Johnny had to leave in a wheelchair and stay off his leg for at least a week. Then crutches could be used until the wounds healed. The boys would have to return to the hospital in one week to check their progress. The boys rode home in the cab of the pickup and Johnny's father sat in the bed of the truck, in the wheelchair. They stopped at the vet's on the way home. Dr. Penegore asked Johnny's father to come into his operating room. Dr. Penegore wanted him to look at Butch. Butch's flesh was ripped down to the bone on one side. Dr. Penegore asked Johnny's father if he wanted Butch put to sleep. Johnny's father said, "If here's any chance of saving him, I want you to do it." Dr. Penegore had sedated Butch, cleaned his wounds and stitched them closed. "I'll give him an injection of antibiotics and hope for the best," said Dr. Penegore. Johnny's father picked Butch up, put him in a cardboard box that the vet gave him and carried him to the pickup. Johnny's father told him that Butch was still alive and they would just have to wait to see if he survives. "Butch gave me time to get my rifle out and get a shot at the bear, so he deserves to live," said Uncle Seth. "If it hadn't been for Butch, one of you might have been killed," said Johnny's father.

The next day, the boys went back to the river to retrieve their belongings. The bear had eaten all their fish and had scattered the remains of their lunch everywhere. Sam said, "The next time we go fishing we'll carry a gun and stay on the bank of the river instead of walking through it."

A few days after Butch's injuries, he opened his eyes and gave a weak little whine. Johnny knelt down on the floor beside Butch, reached down in the cardboard box where Butch was lying and petted his head. Butch tried to raise himself up, but was still too weak. Instead, he just whined and licked Johnny's hand. Johnny looked at Butch and said in a low, tender voice, "Hey, Pal, thanks for saving our lives. I'm sorry you got so hurt by that bear. I guess you're going to be okay now." Johnny's mother came in and said, "I'm glad to see that Butch is doing a little better. I made him some chicken broth and will feed him with an eye dropper in a few minutes." Johnny said, "Thanks Mother, Butch and I appreciate you." Just then, Johnny's father came in from the woods and said, "Well, look who's getting better. It looks like dogs can have nine lives as well as cats!" Butch sensed that all this attention was for him and he managed to wag his tail a little bit. In a couple of weeks, Butch was back to his old self again, running and jumping like nothing had ever happened. Everyone was grateful to see Butch's full recovery, as they all loved him very much.

School would be out in a couple of weeks and summer vacation would begin. The boys were anxious for the school year to end, as they had spring fever. Spring fever was the longing to be outdoors on the warm, sunny days, before school let out for the summer. "We've got a lot of work to do both on the farms and in the woods this summer," said Johnny. "You're right," said Sam. "But I want to look for that lost gold mine in the mountains this summer." "We'll go as soon as we can get some time off from our chores," said Johnny. The boys made their plans and were ready to go find gold at the first opportunity.

CHAPTER 2
GOLD FEVER

"Let's go gold hunting," hollered Johnny, as he pulled his car alongside Sam's barn. Sam was sitting in the barn doorway waiting for Johnny to come pick him up and replied, "You betcha!" "Let's find lots of gold nuggets and get rich because I'm sick and tired of milking these cows every day of my life," laughed Sam. With loud music playing on the car radio, the boys headed down the red dirt road, excited to be going on their new adventure.

Daylight was just breaking in the horizon and dew was still glittering on the ground. It was a perfect day to look for gold; the sky was clear and there was a chill in the air, but would warm up soon. "I have a feeling that we're going to find some gold on this trip," said Johnny with a big grin on his face. "I'm excited, said Sam; I can't wait to get there and start panning."

The boys reached the end of the red dirt country road and prepared to start climbing the looming mountain before them. Although this mountain range was a little over two thousand feet high, it was very steep, rugged, and would be hard to climb. Johnny had heard stories all his life about gold having been found, long ago, in this area. There were reports of Indians having used gold nuggets to trade for supplies in the past. Also, it was said that the Indians were very secretive as to where they found the gold and they never allowed outsiders in their territory. The Indians had moved out of this area more than two hundred years ago. As time passed, a few prospectors searched these mountain ranges with high hopes of finding the lost Indian gold, but never did, to anyone's knowledge. For the most part, gold hunting in this area had been abandoned a long time ago.

With backpacks full of food, medical supplies, rope, and a couple of pie pans, the boys were ready to go. Sam carried the shovel and Johnny carried a shotgun, in case they encountered any bears, mountain lions, or wolves.

I think we should follow this creek up the mountain," said Johnny. "Good idea," replied Sam. "That way, it'll be a more gradual climb," said Johnny. Johnny took a compass reading and said to Sam, "We'll be going in a northeast direction, so we will come back in a southwest direction." "We need to go where the terrain is the most rugged and in places that most people would have avoided," said Sam. "Good idea," said Johnny. The prospectors would have checked the most accessible areas, hoping to find a quick bonanza."

Following along the banks of the clear, bubbling brook, was easy going. After an hour of walking, the boys came to a clearing along the side of the brook. "It looks like a narrow valley through the mountains," said Sam. "It looks very interesting and I think we should explore that valley," said Johnny.

The green valley was almost treeless and had a slight grade uphill. Johnny kept tying red ribbon to the bushes every fifty yards. This way, the boys could find their way back. They had left the stream behind and the walking was getting harder, due to the large boulders that had fallen off the cliffs. So far, no wildlife had been seen with the exception of a lone, bald eagle gliding overhead. Walking a mile up the valley, the boys came to a steep drop-off of about thirty feet. This was an opening to a larger valley with a small lake in the middle. Tying knots in their rope and securing it to a large rock, the boys lowered themselves into the valley. With the rope attached to the large rock, they could climb out of the valley when they returned.

"Let's start looking for gold in this valley," said Johnny. "I'm hungry," said Sam. "Let's go down by the lake and take a coffee break." "Okay, replied Johnny; I'm always ready to stop and eat!" A small stream was feeding the lake, but there wasn't a stream running out of it. It must go underground, thought Johnny. The water in the stream, feeding the lake, was cold and clear.

The sun was shining and there was not a cloud in the sky. What a beautiful day, thought Johnny. Sam gathered wood and started a small fire for coffee, while Johnny filled the coffee pot with the clear water from the stream. "I wonder if there are any trout in this lake," asked Johnny? "After we eat and look for gold, we can try fishing later in the day," said Sam.

The homemade bread, butter and cheese sandwiches, along with the thin sugar cookies that Johnny's mother had made, tasted good with the steaming, hot coffee. The lake was powder blue and clear as a bell. After the coffee break, the boys started searching for gold along the stream. The boys, having learned how to pan for gold from a book, proceeded to shovel sand and gravel into their pie pans. They picked the rocks and large gravel out of their pans. Johnny thought he could see gold in the bottom of his pan. He took out his magnet and ran it over the shiny flakes and they clung to it. It was just iron pyrite (fool's gold). It looked like gold but was shiny iron crystals. Further up the creek, Sam ended up with a few gold flakes in his pan. The boys paned the stream all the way up to the mountain cliffs.

"Well, let's try our luck at fishing," said Johnny, as he slung the shovel over his shoulder. Fishing line, hooks and sinkers were always in the boys' backpacks. They dug for worms with the shovel, to use for bait. There weren't any small saplings to use for fishing poles on this side of the lake. The boys picked up their backpacks and walked to the other side of the lake where there was a grove of trees.

"It looks like there are plenty of good fishing poles here," said Sam, as he cut down two small saplings for himself and Johnny. "The last one to catch a fish has to do the cooking," teased Johnny. The boys flung their lines into the lake and as soon as the bait hit the water, Johnny had a fish on his line. "I got one," yelled Johnny, as he pulled in a nice eleven-inch long, speckled brook trout. Sam caught one about the same size right after Johnny. The boys each caught another trout and decided that would be enough for lunch. In their backpacks, they also carried an aluminum frying pan, some shortening, salt and pepper for cooking purposes. Johnny gathered some wood and built a fire while Sam was cleaning and preparing the fish.

Johnny wandered back into the woods to see the extent of the grove of trees. He came back and told Sam that there was a lot of forest behind the grove of trees and he didn't see any cliffs. The fresh, golden fried fish tasted great and then the boys decided to explore the forest behind the grove of trees. It was just past noon, so the boys figured a couple of hours could be spent looking in the forest. Their trail was marked with red ribbons to find their way back. Entering the forest, Johnny took a compass reading back toward the lake. It showed the lake was due north.

The boys speculated that this was an area that few prospectors would have been because of having to get down the steep cliffs to reach it. Maybe the Indians had scaled the cliffs using ladders made from the narrow pine trees. Sam and

Johnny felt excited at the thought that this could be the secret place where the Indians had found gold, long ago.

The older trees in this area were tall, virgin white pine, almost two hundred feet high. They were seven to eight feet across the trunks and twenty-five feet around. There was very little growth of small trees, or underbrush, in this area, as the tall trees blocked out the sunlight. The signs of animals were the droppings and hoof prints of deer. There were no birds to be seen, or heard beneath these tall pines. It was very quiet and dark, giving a person an uneasy feeling.

A faint roar could be heard if one was still and listened. As Sam and Johnny walked through the woods, the roar became louder. The forest soon opened up and there was the source of the roar. It was a majestic waterfall about fifty feet high. What a beautiful sight to see! It must have been fed by the water coming from the lake. A large pool of water had formed below the waterfall. This creek would be interesting to pan, as it had run underground for at least a mile. It was late in the afternoon, so the boys decided to go back to the lake, spend the night and explore the creek the next day.

Back at the lake, the boys gathered firewood for the night and made some coffee to go with their cheese and homemade bread. Lying on their packs by the warm fire, the boys gazed at the brilliance of the stars, in the moonless sky. There was one sound that broke the silence and it was the hoot of an owl. The boys were tired and fell asleep, thinking about where they would pan for gold in the morning. Toward morning, Sam added some more wood to the fire which took the chill out of the air.

The boys were up by daybreak, sitting around their camp fire and enjoying fresh, hot coffee and smoked summer sausage sandwiches for their breakfast. They were looking forward to their day. When they were finished eating, Sam walked over to the lake, filled the coffee pot with water, came back and put out the fire. "Let's pack up our stuff and go find some gold," said Sam. With their packs on their backs and the shovels and rifle across their shoulders, they headed for the waterfall. It was an easy climb down to the clear, blue pool at the bottom of the waterfall. "Maybe there's gold in this shallow water right under the waterfall," said Johnny. "Let's get the pie pans out and start shoveling," said Sam. After an hour of hard digging and panning under the waterfall with no results, the boys decided to stop searching this spot. Deflated, the boys decided to follow the creek downstream and pan along the way. It was about noon when the boys realized that this was not the place where the Indians had found their gold nuggets. They decided to go back to the car and try another area, at another time.

By the time the boys got back to the lake, it was mid-afternoon, warm and sunny. Taking a short rest, the boys went back to the cliff where the knotted rope was hanging. It was a thirty-foot climb up the rope to the top of the cliff. "I'll go first and pull up the back packs," said Sam. He was about ten feet from the top when the rope came loose from the rock overhead. Sam tumbled down the cliff and landed in some bushes. He got all scratched up, but not hurt. After applying peroxide and iodine to his scratches and wrapping gauze around his arms and legs, Sam said, "I'm okay and ready to go." "We can't get out this way and will have to find another way through the tall pines," said Johnny.

"If you follow a creek downstream, it will lead you to a road and to civilization," said Johnny. "That's right," agreed Sam. "At least we have nice weather and we know we're headed south from the lake," said Johnny. "That means we should be going in the direction of the car," said Sam. Following the creek south the boys came out of the tall pines and into the hardwood forest.

The sounds to be heard were chirping birds and chattering squirrels. "How are your scratches doing," asked Johnny? "They still sting a little and I feel achy from the fall. I know I'll have some bad bruises by tomorrow, but am lucky I didn't break anything," said Sam. "I was scared when you fell and I was afraid you had hurt yourself," replied Johnny.

After following the stream for an hour, Sam said, "I'm going to pan here to check for gold," He dug under some rocks, piled dirt into his pan and swished it around, checking for nuggets. Much to his disappointment, a few tiny flakes of gold were found. This is such back-breaking, hard work; let's do something else," said Sam. "It's getting late. Let's go," replied Johnny.

Rounding a turn in the creek, the boys were looking at low mountains with cliffs, thirty to forty feet high. "There's no way to climb up those cliffs," said Johnny. Following the creek toward the cliffs, the stream disappeared into the ground. Where the creek stopped, there was no way to continue through these mountains without scaling another high cliff. "What should we do now," asked Johnny? "I think I can climb that little cliff over there. It has some jagged areas where I can get good hand and foot holds," said Sam. "If you don't make it going up that cliff, there aren't any bushes down here to break your fall," said Johnny. "If we could find a dead tree, we could drag it over here and climb up the branches," said Johnny.

"I saw a dead Tamarac not far from here; maybe we can push it over and drag it here," said Sam. The boys walked back to the tree that Sam had mentioned. After thirty minutes of trying to push it over, they decided it was not going to topple over. "Let's cut some small saplings down with our hunting knives, cut our rope in pieces, and make a ladder," said Johnny. Using their knives, the boys cut down some saplings and dragged them over to the cliff. "We'll have to put the big ones on the bottom for support," said Sam.

When the forty-foot ladder was ready, it was too heavy to lift. "We'll have to take the top twenty feet off," said Johnny. "We'll lean the bottom half of the ladder against the cliff and build the top half as we go up," said Sam. That's the plan the boys followed and it worked just fine. The boys had used all their rope on the ladder and hoped that no more cliffs would have to be scaled. "If we had thought of it, we could have built a ladder at the bottom of the cliff where you fell," said Johnny. "If we'd done that we would be back at the car by now eating a sandwich," replied Sam. Time was being used up and it was already late afternoon when Sam said, "I hope we can get out of here before dark."

There weren't any trees; just bushes on this narrow trail between the mountain walls. After winding through these low mountains for a mile, the narrow trail opened up and a small canyon appeared in front of the boys. Without a cliff to scale, the boys walked down into the canyon. There were several exits out of the canyon and no cliffs in sight. "Take a compass reading so we can decide which exit to use," said Sam. Johnny reached into his pocket and pulled out his compass. The needle was going in circles and Johnny shook it to make it stop. "The needle keeps going in a circle," said Johnny. "There must be a lot of iron deposits in this canyon rock," said Sam. "The compass is useless," said Johnny. "The sun is going down so we can tell which way is west," said Sam. "I think we should go out that exit to the west," said Johnny. "It's going to be dark in a few hours, so I think we should stay in this canyon tonight," said Sam.

There was a small grove of trees in the center of the canyon. "I'll gather wood for a fire," said Sam. "I'll go with you and maybe we can find some water for coffee," said Johnny. The boys had grown up drinking coffee and always carried it in their back packs; it was easy to make and was a nice, comforting, hot, beverage.

Just after entering the grove of trees, sure enough, there was a spring bubbling up out of the ground. Johnny bent over to get water with the coffee pot when something caught his eye. It was a shiny, gold colored pebble, right on the bank of the spring. Johnny picked it up and thought to himself, could this be gold? He called Sam over, who was carrying an armful of wood, and said, "Look at this, Sam, do you think its gold?" Sam's eyes grew wide with excitement, as he dropped the wood on the ground. Sam snatched the pebble from Johnny's hand and said, "I think it is!" Sam pulled out his pen knife, pressed it into the pebble and said, "It's soft, so it must be gold." I think this is where the Indians must have gotten their gold nuggets," said Sam. The boys threw off their backpacks, pulled out their pie pans and began shoveling dirt from the bank of the spring. They dipped the coffee pot into the spring to wash the dirt in their pans. They were careful not to muddy up their drinking and coffee water. "Wow, exclaimed Sam!" He was seeing gold flakes and a few small nuggets, the size of apple seeds, in his pan. Johnny ended up with the same exciting results in his pan as well. "We're going to be rich," exclaimed Johnny! "I can't believe we've found the lost Indian gold," said Sam. "First, we have to find our way out of here," said Johnny. Leaving the gold in their pans, the boys gathered the wood that Sam had dropped when he saw the gold nugget, and made a fire. Sam made the coffee and it tasted good with the last of the bread and cheese. The boys spent the night in the canyon but were too excited to sleep. They talked all through the night about how rich they were going to be and how much good they would do for their families, friends, and community with all the money they would get from the gold they would find tomorrow. A few clouds floated by in the starry sky, as the boys lay awake by the crackling fire. Wolves started howling up on the ridge of the canyon. Johnny pulled his shotgun closer and Sam got up and put more wood on the fire. Toward morning, the boys sank into deep sleep, thinking about the gold they had found.

The next morning, the boys awoke to a cloudy sky and drizzling rain. The hot coffee and the last of their smoked summer sausage tasted so good. With the shovel and pie pans, the boys headed for the spring to pan for some more gold. More gold flakes showed up in their pans, along with an abundance of small nuggets. The drizzle was getting heavier so the boys decided that they had better make their way out of the canyon. They took the exit that they had determined was west by the setting sun. The gold was put in the coffee pot for safekeeping. The boys decided to come back to the canyon with real gold pans and get a lot of gold later. Excited about their discovery, the boys couldn't stop grinning and talking about the things they would buy with their new found wealth. Once outside the canyon, Johnny thought about marking their trail with red ribbon, but decided against it. If someone came across their trail of red ribbon, they could follow it to the canyon and to the gold. Instead, he would trust his compass which was now working okay. Outside the canyon was a hardwood forest, but no streams were visible anywhere. Every hundred yards

Johnny checked his compass to make sure they were walking toward the west.

The sky turned dark and the drizzle turned into a harder rainfall. Going down a hill Johnny slipped and went tumbling head over heels. He lost his backpack on the way down along with the shotgun. He didn't get hurt and retrieved his backpack and shotgun. At the bottom of the hill, Johnny decided to check their direction with his compass but it had come out of his pocket during the tumble. "I lost the compass," hollered Johnny. "Let's go look for it," replied Sam. They searched everywhere for the compass but couldn't find it. Now it had started raining harder and the sky was getting darker; they abandoned the search and took shelter under a spruce tree's wide, thick branches.

The boys decided they would try to walk in a straight line using three points lined up in a row. They also started using the red ribbon to mark their trail and hoped they were walking west. After two hours of walking in the rain, Sam said, "I see a red ribbon up ahead." The boys had walked in a large circle and were now lost. They sat down to rest. The rain was beginning to let up and the dark clouds seemed to be moving away now. The sky cleared and became blue again. The North Star was visible and the boys were able to use it as a guiding light to begin walking in a southwestern direction.

Three hours later, the now exhausted boys stumbled onto an abandoned railroad track. They decided to take a rest. They laid on their backpacks and fell asleep. They were awakened by the nearby howl of wolves. By the light of the starry sky, along with the moon,

Johnny could see the figures of a pack of wolves coming in their direction. Johnny fired a shot into the air with his shotgun, but the wolves didn't scatter. Sam was standing up holding the shovel to do battle with the wolves. The wolves didn't run when Johnny fired the shotgun over their heads which concerned Johnny. "Sam, we have a problem. I think we have a pack of rabid wolves coming after us," said Johnny. "Healthy wolves would have scattered after you shot in their direction," said Sam. "They've got us surrounded, so we can't get off the railroad bed and climb a tree," said Johnny. "We will just have to fight them," said Sam. As the wolves came in range of the shotgun, Johnny fired, knocking down the first wolf. Johnny re-loaded the shotgun, firing at another growling wolf, killing him. Johnny was able to re-load one more time and fire, hitting he third wolf. Johnny got out his hunting knife and swung it at a leaping wolf with his fangs bared. The wolf was going for Johnny's throat, as the knife plunged into the wolf's side. Sam had disabled two wolves with the shovel, but another wolf had plunged his teeth into Sam's arm. Johnny lunged at the wolf attacking Sam and killed it with his knife. The remaining wolves in the pack ran into the woods. All the wolves were foaming at the mouth, so they had rabies and Sam had been bitten. "Did you get bitten, asked Sam?" "I don't think so," said Johnny. "I see blood on your shirt near your shoulder," said Sam. Johnny took off his shirt and sure enough, the wolf that had leaped at Johnny's throat had nicked his shoulder with his teeth. "Looks like both of us are going to get rabies shots," said Johnny.

The railroad track seemed to be running in an east and west direction. "I think we should follow the railroad track to the west," said Sam. It was breaking daylight when the boys found a dirt road crossing the bed of the old railroad track. Tracks of one vehicle were imprinted on the road, in the red clay. Those tracks look like my big mud and snow tires," said Johnny. "In which direction do you think the car is," asked

Sam? "I think it's to the right; I remember that odd-shaped tree hanging over the road," said Johnny. "Oh, yes, it was on my side of the car when we drove under it," said Sam. It feels good to walk on a bare road," said Johnny. The sun was just rising over the treetops and the day looked like it was going to be sunny and warm.

Leaving their backpacks and shovel alongside the road, the boys started walking toward the car. Coming around a curve in the road, thirty minutes later, the boys saw a wonderful site: the car! Johnny packed the shotgun in the car trunk and headed down the road to pick up their backpacks and shovel.

"I can't believe we found gold," said Sam. I almost forgot about the gold," said Johnny. "I was more worried about getting back to civilization." "I don't think we could find our way back to that canyon from the way we came out; however, we could find it from the way we went in," said Sam.

Sam dozed on the way back home and awoke when Johnny pulled into his driveway. Sam's father was outside working on a tractor; Johnny and Sam went to show him their gold. Pouring the gold onto the lid of the coffee pot, Sam's father said, "Well, it looks like you boys found some gold!" "Sam, why are you all scratched up and bandaged," asked Sam's father? "I fell while I was scaling a cliff when the rope let loose, tumbling me into some bushes. I'm okay, but will have a few bruises tomorrow," said Sam.

"Where did you find this gold," asked Sam's father? "It was near a spring in a canyon," said Sam. "We plan to go back with real gold pans and get more gold," said Sam. You can go back for a couple of days, but you need to be here to harvest the hay," said Sam's father.

"We were attacked by rabid wolves and were bitten," said Johnny. "You will have to take the rabies shots. We better get you to the hospital right away, as they keep anti-rabies medicine on hand," said Sam's father. Sam's father drove both boys to the hospital for the shots. The boys explained to the doctor what had happened with the pack of wolves. The doctor said they would have to take a series of six shots in the stomach and they would hurt. The boys gasped when they saw the long needles that were going to be used. "These syringes with the serum will prevent you from getting rabies," said the doctor. The shot hurt a lot and the boys weren't looking forward to the next five. The bite marks were doctored and the boys were released to go home.

"We still need to make a rope ladder," said Sam. "Okay," said Johnny. "I'll come back this evening and help you." Taking the coffee pot with him, Johnny wanted to show his father the gold. Johnny's father had just come home from the woods for lunch. Johnny pulled his car into the yard and got out the coffee pot. When Johnny entered the kitchen, his father said, "Did you find any gold?" "Sure did," said Johnny, as he opened the coffee pot and poured the gold into the lid. Johnny's father was surprised when he saw the gold. His father tested it with a sharp knife and said, "That's real gold!" "Sam and I want to make one more trip back to a spring, in the middle of a hidden canyon where we found the gold," said Johnny. "Okay, said his father, but then you have to help me haul some logs to the paper mill when you get back."

"Sam and I were attacked by rabid wolves and Sam's father took us to the hospital to start a series of anti-rabies shots. We were both bitten by the wolves. All the wolves were foaming at the mouth and had no fear of the shotgun. We killed six then the rest of the pack ran away," said Johnny. "It was good that you had the shotgun; otherwise, the pack would have killed both you and Sam. I'm glad you boys both made it through that ordeal. You don't have to go into the woods to work until you're ready," said Johnny's father. Johnny knew an old man who had prospected for gold in Alaska who might have some real gold pans. He went to see the old man and knocked on his door. "Come in," said the old man who was in his nineties. "I came to see if you have any gold pans that I could borrow," said Johnny. The old man replied, "My name's Ed Masterson, please call me Ed" "Thanks Ed, I'm happy to make your acquaintance after all these years," replied Johnny with a big grin on his face. Ed said, "Well, what in the world do you need gold pans for?" Johnny related his story to Ed about his and Sam's discovery of gold in the hidden canyon. Then he went out to his car and got the coffee can with the gold in it to show to Ed. After examining the nuggets, Ed said, "This is the real stuff." Johnny went on to say that they had found the gold around a spring in a canyon and thought they had found the source of the   legendary Indians' gold.

"Maybe you have and maybe you haven't," said Ed, with a twinkle in his pale blue eyes. "What do you mean," asked Johnny? Ed said, "The spring may have been a stopping off place for the Indians and maybe they lost some of their gold while they were getting water from the spring. I hope for your sake that you have found the source of the Indians' gold, as it could make you very rich. I wish you boys well, but don't get your hopes up too high yet. My advice to you is to pan some more around the spring to see if you continue to find nuggets. If you stop finding them, it is not the source." Then Ed went on to confide to Johnny that twenty years ago, he too had gone off in search for the elusive Indians' gold, in those same mountains; however, he was too old to scale those cliffs and had abandoned his search. Ed gave Johnny two gold pans that he had used in his gold panning days. Ed said, "You go ahead and keep these pans. They are a gift from one gold hunter to another. I hope they bring you good luck. I'll be thinking about you boys and wishing I could be going along with you." Johnny thanked Ed and drove over to Sam's farm to help him build the rope ladder. This time they made two sources with which to anchor it in case one tie came loose again.

The next morning, the boys were up before daylight headed back to their secret canyon. Excitement was running high, as the boys stopped the car at the end of the road. This time they took a mason jar with a screw-on lid to fill with gold. The rope ladder was heavy, so it was the one thing that Sam carried, besides his backpack. Johnny carried the pans, shovel, food and the shotgun. Sam's backpack had the coffee pot, coffee grounds, sugar, and the medical supplies in it. The boys followed the same path as before, using the red ribbons as guides to find the cliff. Anchoring one rope from the ladder to the base of a small tree and the other to a large rock, the boys threw the ladder over the side of the cliff. Then they climbed down the ladder, one at a time, to the floor of the valley.

The powder blue lake looked like a brilliant gem with the sun shining on it. A lone eagle was circling above. Walking around the lake, the boys headed into the pine forest. It was very pleasant this time of the morning, as they hiked through the tall, shady pines. It was cool, still and quiet. The one sound they could hear was the crunching of fallen pine cones beneath their boots, as they tramped along the forest floor. Coming out of the pines and following the creek through the hardwoods, the boys came to the cliff where their ladder was standing. They took a short rest then climbed the ladder up the cliff. The boys were excited when they reached the opening to the canyon. "I feel like someone from out of the past, during the gold rush days must have felt just before declaring that he had found a bonanza," said Sam. "This is going to be a great day for us. We're going to be rich," said Johnny.

The boys walked down to the spring, in the grove of trees and got out their gold pans. The spring was quite large, about ten feet across and six feet deep. The water was crystal clear and they could see all the way to the bottom. The dirt around the spring was easy to shovel. The boys made sure that the water in the spring stayed clean by dipping the coffee pot in it, to get water for washing out their gold pans.

Sam was the first to start panning and said, "I've got gold in my pan!" Sure enough, a couple of small nuggets, about the size of apple seeds, gleamed through the sand in Sam's pan. Johnny was more excited, as he had a larger nugget in his first pan. It was about the size of a marble. The boys kept finding gold in the shallow dirt close to the spring; however, when they moved away from the spring, no more gold was found.

Could it be that Ed Masterson, the old prospector, was right about the Indians having spilled some of their gold while getting water out of the spring? The boys searched the canyon in different places, even though they didn't find any more gold. After having some hot coffee and ham sandwiches, they decided that this was not the source of the Indians' gold. The boys had recovered about three ounces of gold which was nice, but not a bonanza. Sam said, "The gold must be in this area, since we found some at the spring."

It was mid-afternoon so the boys figured they should start back to the car while it was still daylight. Disappointed at not having found the source of the Indians' gold, the boys agreed they would search again in the future. They would have to wait until fall to try again, as they were needed back home for harvesting and working in the woods. It had been a fun adventure and exciting when they had found gold at the spring.

On the way back to the car, Sam spotted a bunch of wild raspberry bushes and said to Johnny, "Let's stop and eat some berries." Johnny agreed, as the bushes were loaded with the sweet red fruit. After eating all the berries they could hold, the boys started to leave the berry patch. Sam yelled, "I've been stung by some bees!" Johnny got stung as well, but they weren't bees; they were hornets. The boys ran from the patch with a swarm of mad hornets in close pursuit. After a short while, the hornets gave up their chase. The boys had been stung on their faces, neck and hands. "These stings hurt," said Sam. "Yes, they do. Let's get to the creek and put some cold mud on them," said Johnny. The mud from the creek took some of the pain away, as it drew out a little of the poison. "You look like a monster," Sam told Johnny. The boys' faces had swelled up with large bumps caused by the stings. "You look pretty bad yourself," said Johnny. Even though they were in pain, they laughed at each other with the gobs of mud all over their necks and faces. "We had better get going. We're still a half mile from the car," said Johnny. Sam stood up on the creek bank, grabbed his throat and said, "I'm having hard time breathing."

"What do you mean," asked Johnny? "I feel like my throat is closing up," said Sam. "We had better hurry back to the car and get you to a hospital," said Johnny. "Okay. Let's go," said Sam. The boys started down the trail to the car, but Sam was falling behind. "Hurry up," yelled Johnny, as he looked back at Sam. Sam was weaving and then fell to the ground. Johnny ran back to Sam whose face was turning blue. "Johnny, I can't breathe," gasped Sam. "You'll have to cut my windpipe, or I'll die," murmured Sam. Johnny was frozen in horror at what Sam just said. "Do it! Hurry," whispered Sam. Johnny had read a story about someone who had suffered a severe allergic reaction to a bee sting that had caused his throat to close up and his friend had cut his windpipe to save his life. Sam was wheezing trying to get some air and Johnny knew he had to do something fast. Johnny had a ballpoint pen in his backpack. He took the pen apart and cut one end of the barrel to stick into Sam's windpipe. He got out the gauze and iodine from his backpack. Johnny fetched water from the creek to wash the mud from Sam's face and throat; then washed the mud off his hands as well. Johnny sterilized the knife blade and his hands with iodine. "Hold on, Buddy," said Johnny, but there was no response from Sam. Sam was unconscious and gasping for air. Johnny hurried and brushed Sam's lower neck with iodine and was feeling for his windpipe. Johnny stuck his pocket knife into Sam's throat. Blood squirted everywhere and he thought he had cut a major vein; then, the blood began to flow slower. Johnny stuck his fingers in the open cut feeling for the windpipe. He felt Sam's windpipe in his fingers. He cut through it with his pen knife and a gush of bloody air spurted all over Johnny's face. I have to stick the barrel of the ballpoint pen into the windpipe, thought Johnny. The windpipe had collapsed, as Sam's lungs were trying to suck in air. Johnny squeezed the windpipe about an inch from the cut and was able to stick the pen barrel into it. Johnny could now feel Sam's lungs pumping air in and out through the pen. Sam was still alive. Johnny wrapped a strip of gauze around the windpipe to hold the pen in place. Blood was still spurting all over, so Johnny plugged the open cut with gauze and poured iodine over it. The blood flow slowed down, but was still oozing out of the gauze. Johnny wrapped more strips of gauze around Sam's neck to hold everything in place. Sam was too heavy for Johnny to carry so he had to drag Sam over a quarter of a mile to the car. Johnny had to stop every twenty-five yards to rest even though the trail was downhill. Soon the car was in sight. Relieved, Johnny pulled Sam to the car and got him inside. Sam was covered in blood but was still breathing. Sam's face was pale, as he had lost a lot of blood. Johnny thought he would bleed to death, or his heart would stop due to lack of blood. Johnny covered Sam with a blanket from the trunk. Then he closed Sam's door, ran around the car and jumped in the driver's seat. He reached in his pocket for the keys but they weren't there. Johnny was breathless with anxiety. This was a matter of life or death! Maybe I dropped them around the creek when we were putting the cold mud on our faces, thought Johnny. Racing back up to the creek where they had stopped, Johnny looked for the keys. There they were, in the shallow creek, under about a foot of water. Relieved to find the keys, Johnny washed his bloody hands off in the creek. Johnny's legs were in pain from dragging Sam to the car, but he ran as fast as he could all the way back. Johnny swung the car door open and slid into the seat. When Johnny stuck the key into the ignition nothing happened. The battery was dead. That's when Johnny noticed that the lights had been left on the whole time they had been gone. Johnny's heart sank when he realized that Sam would die before he could get back with help. Sam already looked close to death; his breathing was labored and his face was pale.

Johnny tried to push the car to get it started, but the road was too wet and it wouldn't budge. Then he heard the groan of a large truck engine. It was coming out of the woods loaded down with heavy logs. Johnny hurried to get his shotgun out of the trunk and fired a shot into the air, hoping the driver would hear it. He saw the brake lights come on, as the truck came to a stop; then it started moving again. Johnny put another shell in the gun and fired again. This time, the truck stopped and the driver got out. It was Kurt Hawkins, who owned a local trucking company. Johnny took off his shirt and started waving it in the air. Mr. Hawkins got back into the truck and backed it onto the logging road. Then he pulled onto the gravel road in Johnny's direction. Johnny's heart raced, as he saw the big logging truck coming toward him. Mr. Hawkins stopped his truck behind Johnny's car and got out. "What's the problem," he asked? Johnny explained what had happened to Sam and that he needed to get to a hospital fast. Mr. Hawkins went over to Johnny's car and took a look at Sam. "He must have lost a lot of blood because he's so pale," said Mr. Hawkins. "Let's get him into my truck." With Sam and Johnny in the truck cab, Mr. Hawkins turned the groaning truck around and headed down the gravel road. He called the sheriff's office on his CB radio. He told them that he needed an escort to the nearest hospital. He asked the operator who answered the phone at the sheriff's office, to notify the hospital emergency room staff that he was on his way with a bleeding person, suffering from an allergic reaction to hornet stings and a cut windpipe.

The truck had a full load of logs, including a trailer. Mr. Hawkins didn't want to take time to unhitch the load of logs, as time was of the essence. The truck was moving fast down the gravel road and Mr. Hawkins was blowing the loud diesel truck horns at every corner. A deputy sheriff was waiting where the gravel road ended and the pavement began. With the lights flashing and the siren screaming, Mr. Hawkins followed the deputy's car. The deputy cleared the road for the big truck with its load of logs all the way to the hospital emergency room.

Hospital attendants were waiting with a stretcher on wheels, at the emergency entrance. They lifted Sam onto the stretcher and wheeled him into the hospital. "Take him to Operating

Room B," shouted the doctor on duty. The doctor told a nurse to take Sam's blood pressure. When the nurse told the doctor the results, the doctor said, "His blood pressure is too low to operate." "Take his blood sample and get it typed in the lab as soon as possible," ordered the doctor. The doctor asked Johnny what had happened. Johnny explained everything to him. "If you hadn't cut his windpipe, he would be dead right now," said the doctor to Johnny. "How did you know how to do a Tracheotomy procedure," asked the doctor? I had read an article a while back in *Wilderness* magazine about two people in this same situation," said Johnny. "I felt sick to my stomach when I did it but I knew in my heart that it was Sam's last chance," said Johnny. "It wasn't perfect but it worked and you did save his life," said the doctor. "We have to get some blood in him real soon, or he will have a heart attack and die," said the doctor.

The nurse came back with the lab results on Sam's blood work and she had a very concerned look on her face. His blood type is B-Positive, said the nurse, and we don't have any." "It will take about three hours to get some here from another hospital," said the nurse. "That's too long. He must have a blood transfusion within the hour, or, I'm afraid he won't make it," replied the doctor. "Do you know if anyone on the staff has B-Positive blood," asked the doctor?" "None that I know of," said the nurse.

Johnny spoke up and said, "I have B-Positive blood." The doctor and nurse looked at each other and the doctor asked Johnny, "How old are you?" "How old do I have to be to give blood," asked Johnny? "The hospital requires that you be at least sixteen and have your parents' approval," said the doctor. "Well, I'm sixteen, said Johnny and my parents would approve." Johnny was fourteen and hated telling this little "white" lie, but this was a special case and his best friend's life was at risk. "You will have to sign a form giving us your permission to draw your blood," said the nurse. "Your parents will also have to sign the form and we'll need to call them for their verbal approval," said the nurse "We don't have a phone on the farm," said Johnny, but I'll get them to sign it later."

The doctor gave a worried glance to the nurse and said, "Under the circumstances, I think we should do it now." The nurse agreed and told Johnny since he was so young, he would have to stay overnight in the hospital and have his blood pressure watched. Johnny was told to go and clean up in the bathroom and put on a hospital gown. Then he was put on a rolling bed and wheeled into a room where his blood was drawn. Johnny felt a little lightheaded after his blood had been taken and was given a glass of orange juice to settle his system. Then he was wheeled into a hospital room where he was served a good, hot meal, on a tray in bed.

Johnny was in a room with two beds but the other bed was empty. He got so comfortable, warm and relaxed, he dosed off to sleep. He was awakened a little while later by a nurse who wanted to take his blood pressure. The doctor came in to see Johnny and said that Sam was going to be all right. The doctor reached into his pocket and pulled out the barrel of the pen that Johnny had stuck into Sam's windpipe. "I thought you would like to keep this as a souvenir," said the doctor. "The surgery went well and Sam is now in the recovery room," said the doctor. When he wakes up, we will move him into this room with you," said the nurse. It was around midnight when they brought Sam into the room with Johnny. He was awake and had some color in his cheeks. When Sam spotted Johnny in the other bed he grinned and gave Johnny a thumbs up. The nurse hovered around Sam for a while, taking his blood pressure and checking his bandage. Then, she shut the lights off and left the room. The boys were awakened the next morning for a blood pressure check and Sam had his bandage changed. Johnny had a good breakfast, served to him in bed, at the hospital. However, Sam had an IV stuck in a vein to give him nourishment and to keep him stabilized. Johnny was told he could get dressed and go home after breakfast. However, Sam would have to stay in the hospital for a few days.

Johnny's clothes had been washed and he got dressed. Before leaving, he went by to say goodbye to Sam. He said, "Sam, we are now blood brothers; you have my blood running through your veins. Sam made a funny face and pretended like he was choking. Then Sam grinned and grabbed Johnny's hand and shook it. "See you in a few days," said Johnny as he went out the door. A deputy sheriff was waiting for Johnny at the checkout desk. The deputy came to give Johnny a ride back to his car and would help him start it. Johnny saw the doctor who had helped them, on the way out of the hospital and thanked him again. "We got in touch with Sam's parents and they are on the way to the hospital to see him," said the doctor.

When Johnny got back to his car, the backpacks and shovel were in the back seat. The truck driver, Mr. Hawkins, had walked back up to the creek and had brought the backpacks and shovel to the car. There was a note on the dashboard from Mr. Hawkins saying that he had charged up the battery so the car should start. When Johnny turned the key in the ignition, his car started. Johnny thanked the deputy for the ride and headed home. Johnny stopped his car near the logging road and walked into the woods to thank Mr. Hawkins for saving Sam's life and for all his kindnesses, but he was nowhere to be found. Johnny asked one of the men working on the road where the logging truck driver was. The road worker said that Mr. Hawkins had come in for one load of logs and wouldn't be back for several weeks. Johnny thanked the man for the information and walked back to his car. Johnny was in a good mood driving home because he knew that he and Sam would soon be going on another adventure.

CHAPTER 3
TORNADO'S FURY

It had been a hot, muggy day and huge, dark, billowing clouds could be seen in the distance. It looked like a fierce storm was headed for the area. The rumbling of thunder could be heard and sporadic flashes of lightning could be seen in the sky. The rain would be welcomed to cool off the hot, humid, day.

The local farms were buzzing with activity, preparing the fields for planting and harvesting of grain in the fall. Hay for the animals would be cut and gathered during the summer. Certain chores required entire families to participate during planting and harvesting. Farm boys and girls started driving tractors and farm machinery at a young age. Johnny learned to drive a tractor at the age of eight and his father bought him an old car when he was twelve. Driving was done on the country roads, or on the farms. Even though it was illegal to drive on any road under the age of sixteen, it was accepted in the farm community; driving was limited and with the approval of the parents.

Strong gusts of wind started blowing and the rain began pelting down hard. Johnny said to his dog, Butch, "We'd better get inside before we get drenched!" Lightning bolts hit the ground nearby and a heavy downpour began.

The animals in the barn became very nervous, as the hail started riddling the tin roof like machine gun fire. The storm lasted well into the night, but when it had passed, the air felt cool and fresh. Sleeping that night was very relaxing and a good night's rest was enjoyed by everyone.

Johnny was awakened the next morning by Butch, just as daylight was breaking. It was Sunday morning and Johnny's day to sleep late. Butch wouldn't leave Johnny alone and kept running between Johnny and the window. Johnny got up to see what was bothering him. He noticed something in the grass moving around, but it wasn't daylight enough to make out what it was. Putting on his clothes, Johnny went outside to investigate. Butch was the first one out the front door and he started barking at the grass. Johnny couldn't believe what he saw, once his eyes became accustomed to the twilight. "Fish," yelled Johnny! There were hundreds of fish in the yard and on the road. The storm must have had a tornado in it, as it passed over rivers and lakes. The fish must have been sucked up by the tornado then dropped, as it passed over the farm country.

Most of the dead fish had been picked up around the farm and were buried in a field. The smell of rotting fish was in the air for a couple weeks until another rainstorm washed the unpleasant odor away.

During breakfast, there was a knock on the kitchen door. It was one of the neighbors who said, "The Johnsons' barn was hit by lightning and it burned to the ground. They got all the animals out, but there is no place to keep them. They need a new barn, or they will have to sell their cows, horses, and pigs," said the neighbor.

An emergency meeting was held at the town hall to see what could be done to help the Johnsons'. One man stood up and said, "It's simple. We'll build them a new barn." Everyone agreed and it was to be done right away. All the materials needed to rebuild the Johnsons' barn, including the labor would be donated by the townspeople.

An old fashioned barn raising was in progress with two shifts of people donating their time and supplies. The men worked on the construction of the barn, while the women took care of the animals and fed the workers. Even the kids carried water, food and supplies to the men building the barn. The new barn was completed in ten days. A celebration followed with music, dancing, and all kinds of mouth-watering food. The festive celebration was, of course, held inside the Johnsons' new barn. It was heartwarming to see the whole community come together, in a time of need. With Mrs. Johnson by his side, Mr. Johnson stood up to express gratitude to everyone, but the words just wouldn't come out. He burst into tears every time he made an attempt to speak. Then people stood up and applauded him. It was plain to see how grateful the Johnsons were; everyone just gathered around them and hugged each other. It was a wonderful party and everyone went home feeling good.

During a morning coffee break, while working harvesting logs, Johnny thought he smelled smoke. It's one of the neighbors burning brush, thought Johnny. Upon arriving home for lunch, Johnny's mother said, "A forest ranger was here and said that a forest fire had started about five miles south of the farm and was moving in this direction." The ranger was out rounding up help to fight the fire. Johnny's father and oldest brother, Scottie, left to go to the ranger station, to be of service.

Johnny's father, who could drive a bulldozer, was needed to push a path through the woods to try and stop the fire. Men, women and older children were also fighting the blaze. However, it was gaining in strength, due to a southwestern wind. From the farm, smoke could be seen on the golden, reddish horizon.

With the roar of the fire getting louder and the smell of smoke getting stronger, it was apparent that the fire was out of control. Late that afternoon, Johnny's father and brother arrived at the farm. "We have to get the cows into the field by the river," said Johnny's father, as the fire has already jumped over the road we pushed through the forest.

The animals were herded down the road to a pasture by the river. The river would serve as a natural firebreak. There were no trees in the pasture to catch on fire. The problem was that a grass fire could be devastating to the animals and the farm. The animals, of course, would use their instinct and get into the river to survive. Johnny's father cut the wire fencing to give access to the river for the animals.

Evening was falling and the roar of the fire was getting louder. Smoke was getting thicker in the air and the sky was red, in the direction of the blaze. The fire was about a mile from the farm and forest animals could be seen scurrying across the pastures, trying to get away from it. While focusing on the fire, no one had noticed the dark clouds forming north of the farm. Johnny's father was the first to notice the looming storm to the north. A loud, steady noise was accompanying the storm. As the forest fire raced toward the farm from the south, the rainstorm was moving down from the north. Johnny, his father and brothers were in the pasture herding the cows toward the river. Dark clouds started to pass overhead and the rain began to fall. Then it started to hail and Johnny's father yelled, "Head for the tin shelter!"

The water tank, used by the cows was under a tin shelter, in the middle of the pasture. It was a large, round, steel tank about ten feet in diameter. Johnny's father and the boys ran and got under the shelter before hail, the size of golf balls, started to come down. The noise from the storm grew louder, like the sound of a freight train and Johnny's father shouted, "Everybody get in the water tank! A tornado is in the storm. Hang onto the inside rail of the tank." The wind increased and the noise grew louder and louder. Then the roof of the tin shelter was ripped off. The windmill which pumped water to the tank blew over with a loud crash. Branches and rocks were hitting the sides of the large tank. The strong circular winds of the tornado were destroying everything in its path. Trees, metal roofing, treetops, rocks and broken boards were flying through the air. The steel tank was starting to move, being pushed by the strong wind. It was dark like night and the roar of the tornado was deafening. The tank was now sliding across the pasture and headed for the river. It hit the barbed wire fence, ripping out the fence posts as it broke the wires.

Hanging on for their lives, Johnny, his brothers and his father had slid across the pasture, to the bank of the river. The tank tipped and started sliding down the bank toward the river. After a rough ride down the bank, the tank hit the river with a splash, throwing Johnny's brothers and father into the river. The water was very cold, but they were able to swim to shore. Johnny's father said, "Where's Johnny?" Johnny's brothers didn't know and they didn't see him in the river. He must still be in the tank," said his father. Johnny's brother, Scottie, swam back to the tank and looked in it. "He's still here in the tank and face down in the water," he yelled. Scottie climbed into the tank and pulled Johnny up out of the water. Johnny's father hollered, "Is he still breathing?" Scottie yelled back, "No, and I need help to get him to shore." Johnny's father and other brother, Eddie, swam out to the tank to pull Johnny to shore. When they reached the shore, Johnny's father said, "We have to get the water out of his lungs." Johnny's father blew air into his mouth and Johnny's brothers pushed on his chest and back to force the water out of Johnny's lungs. After several tries water started to come out of Johnny's mouth, but he still wasn't breathing. "He needs air to his lungs fast, otherwise he'll die," said Johnny's father.

Johnny's father, who was a big, strong man, picked Johnny up off the ground and raised him into the air upside down. With his arms around Johnny's chest, he squeezed Johnny's rib cage forcing more water out of his lungs. "Blow air into his mouth," Johnny's father said. Johnny's brothers blew air into his mouth, then Johnny's father squeezed Johnny's chest again. After a few more tries, Johnny coughed and took in a big breath of air. Johnny coughed a few more times and then started to breathe on his own. Johnny's father laid him down on the river bank and said, "I thought we were going to lose you, but I guess you'll be okay." You have a big bump on your head," said Johnny's brother. "You must have banged your head on the tank, knocking yourself out." After a rest, the boys and their father walked up the river bank in the pouring rain. There were a few cuts and bruises on everyone, but no one suffered any serious injuries.

The cows were still in the river and had come through the storm with a few cuts from flying objects. "Let's go check the house and barns," said Johnny. When they arrived back home, Johnny's mother was on the front porch crying. "What's wrong," asked Johnny's father?" Johnny's mother said that his youngest sister, Janie, was missing. She had gone into the chicken coop to gather eggs just before the storm. The tornado hit the chicken coop and now there was nothing left but rubble in its place. "Let's look for her in the fields; maybe she is still alive," said Johnny's father. "I'll check the woods," said Johnny. Worried and afraid of what they might find, everyone hurried into the fields looking for the young girl. Boards, tin, and dead chickens were scattered everywhere. They searched for hours but couldn't find any sign of her. Walking into the nearby woods, Johnny heard a chicken clucking, but couldn't see it. Johnny listened without breathing and heard the clucking sound coming from up in the trees. Johnny followed the sound to a large oak tree. When he looked up he couldn't believe what he saw. His sister was lying across the end of a large branch near the top of the tree, clutching a chicken. Johnny hollered up to his sister, "Are you okay?" "Yes, just get me down," whimpered his little sister. "Just stay there. I'll be right back," yelled Johnny. He ran home as fast as he could, to tell everyone he had found Janie. "She's in the top of a tree, lying across a large limb, holding on with one hand and clutching a chicken in the other," said Johnny. He told his father that the logging truck's long, hydraulic boom was the best thing that could be raised high enough to get her down, out of the tree. Johnny's father ran to get the logging truck and hurried to the woods. He said, "Somebody has to climb into the bucket on the boom with a rope and tie it around Janie's waist. "I'll go, "said Johnny's oldest sister, Alice. "I can climb from the top of the boom onto the limb and put the rope around her." With a rope around her waist, Alice was raised up on the boom near the large limb; she climbed out onto the limb like a cat. She wrapped her legs around the limb and tied the rope around Janie's waist. She then got back into the bucket on the end of the boom and tied the other end of the rope to it. Johnny's father raised the boom, lifting Janie off the limb. He lowered the girls to the ground.

Johnny's little sister, Janie, was still holding her pet chicken, Pinky, when she reached the ground. She had been in the chicken coop when the hard rain and hail came down. When she heard the loud noise of the tornado, she grabbed her pet chicken, Pinky and crawled under the hens' nests for safety. The walls of the coop exploded and she was sucked up into the tornado. As she was whirling around and around, she thought her life was over when she dropped into the top of the tree. She landed in the branches and fell onto the large limb that she had been holding onto ever since. She had hollered for help many times, but no one could hear her. She didn't think anyone would ever find her up in the top of a tree and she thought she was going to die in that tree top. She was afraid to let go of the limb for fear that she would fall to the ground.

The tornado had climbed the other bank of the river and headed for the forest fire. The fire pushed the tornado back up into the clouds. The rain from the thunderstorm was now putting out the forest fire. A loud hissing sound was heard when the wind, fire, and rain met, sending a large cloud of vapor into the sky. Two of Nature's giants had been in a fierce battle and it was all over in less than an hour.

The cows and other farm animals had been spared from the tornado and forest fire. Some of the other fleeing forest animals were not so lucky. Animals that lived underground were protected from the blazing heat. Other critters found shelter in caves and rivers. Deer were the most vulnerable, since they made their homes in the fields and under the trees. Adult deer could run fast to escape, but the fawns could not keep ahead of the flames.

Johnny's father was curious about the path taken by the tornado and went to investigate. It had cut through the trees like a giant saw. When Johnny's father came home, he was carrying a new-born spotted fawn in his arms. While inspecting the tornado's path of destruction, he heard the cry of the fawn coming from under a spruce tree. The fawn's mother knew that her baby could not outrun the fire and had tried to protect it by placing it under this large spruce tree. The fire had passed close to the fawn's hiding place, singing its fur, but the fawn had been spared. The mother had run on to escape the fire and wouldn't be able to return for her little one.

Johnny's father said, "The little fawn needs milk; get a baby bottle and fill it with fresh cow's milk from the barn." Everyone was overjoyed to have this new little addition and named her Daisy. The little fawn was kept in the barn, but would come into the house when the door was open. She loved to jump up and down on all the beds like a child. "You have to keep Daisy outside," said Johnny's mother. "She might fall off a bed and break a leg." Butch, Johnny's dog, and the deer became best friends and could be seen at times chasing each other through the fields. When the snow started falling, Daisy liked to sleep close to the house, in the tall grass. During the hard, cold winter, she stayed in the warm barn with the cows and horses. Daisy grew into a beautiful doe and after living on the farm for two years, one day, disappeared into the woods.

It was the fall season again. Leaves were turning bright colors of reds, oranges, and yellows. On crisp mornings, the frost would sparkle like diamonds in the bright sunlight. With deer hunting season underway, Johnny feared the worst for Daisy. He missed her very much, as she had become such a part of them. She was a very sociable animal and had no fear of humans. She wouldn't have known to run from the hunters. The hunting season ended with no sign of Daisy.

The snow melted and the beginning of warm spring days had arrived. Johnny and Butch were sitting on the front steps of the house, enjoying the warmth of the sun when Butch jumped up and began staring at the field in front of the house. A deer had come out of the woods with two spotted fawns. "Butch, I think it's Daisy," said Johnny. Butch leaped off the steps and sprinted out into the field to greet them. Butch had just touched noses with Daisy, who had come back to show off her new fawns. "Butch, come back," yelled Johnny. A majestic buck had started to enter the field from the nearby woods. He was the father of the new spotted fawns and was coming to protect them. Butch raced back to the house. Everyone gathered to watch Daisy and her fawns retreat back into the woods. Johnny felt very emotional over Daisy's coming back to show them her babies and to say goodbye for the last time. Although they loved and missed her, they knew it was Nature's way. However, everyone began to feel better when Johnny's mother asked, "Would anyone like to have a piece of hot apple pie with whipped cream on top?"

Johnny started thinking about a fishing trip with Sam, as work in the woods had not yet begun. He would go over and see Sam tomorrow morning.

CHAPTER 4
LAKE MONSTERS

Johnny thought that a bass fishing trip would be great before fall. He went over to see Sam and made the suggestion. "Sure," said Sam. "Why don't we go this coming Saturday?"

A good bass lake was a little over thirty miles away. Too far for bikes, so Johnny would use the old car that his father had bought him. They decided to leave in the afternoon, as bass fishing was best in the evening, just before sunset. Hot dogs and marshmallows were taken to roast over a campfire. The smoky flavor always gave them a delicious taste. Coffee and a coffee pot were brought along to make boiled coffee.

The day was cloudy with the sun's rays peeking between the white, billowing clouds. It seemed like a perfect day for bass fishing. Johnny drove his old car over to Sam's farm and pulled into the driveway. "You ready to go," yelled Johnny? "You betcha," said Sam who was sitting on top of a milk pail in the front yard. "What's the pail for," asked Johnny? "To put our fish in after we catch them," said Sam. "Okay, put your stuff in the car and let's get going," said Johnny. The car had large mud and snow tires on the rear which were good for going through mud holes.

There were no farms or houses along the road to the lake. A few hunting camps, most of which were abandoned, were sprinkled throughout the forest. Stopping at a swampy place along the way, the boys decided to catch some frogs for bait. You had to be very fast to catch a frog by hand, before it jumped or swam away. Spying a frog to catch, Sam crept up behind it and with a quick swoop of his hand, tried to catch it. What appeared to have been a frog with its head out of the water, turned out to be a snake! Startled and wide-eyed at what had just happened, Sam said, "Oh my goodness, I just caught a snake!" Dropping it back into the water, the harmless grass snake slithered off into the weeds. A little leery about catching another snake, Johnny said, "I think we should use artificial lures." "Let's head for the lake," said Sam. "I would rather catch fish than snakes!"

Driving down the winding dirt road to the lake, they spotted two bear cubs playing on the bank of a stream. Johnny drove slow so he wouldn't scare them. Then he came to a quiet stop so he and Sam could enjoy watching the bear cubs wrestling with each other. After watching for a while, Sam said, "Let's catch one" and bolted out of the car before Johnny could say anything. Sam disappeared into the woods in pursuit of the cubs.

"Wait, little bears; I won't hurt you," said Sam, while chasing after the adorable cubs. Johnny saw the cubs scamper to the top of a hemlock tree. With a loud bellow, the mother bear came crashing through the brush, headed straight for the hemlock tree. With the mother bear gaining on Sam, Johnny yelled, "Sam, lookout behind you!" Glancing back, Sam's eyes grew larger when he saw the mother bear coming after him. Johnny started running and yelling at the mother bear. "Sam, get away from the tree," hollered Johnny. Sam ran and dove into a patch of raspberry bushes. With Johnny's running and yelling, the mother bear decided to climb up the tree her cubs were in, to protect them.

Relieved that the mother bear went up the tree, Johnny went to check on Sam. He found him safe in the raspberry patch with a grin on his face. Johnny said, "That was a stupid thing to do." "Whenever you see bear cubs, you know the mother is close by." "You're right," said Sam. "I should have known better." "You're lucky the mother bear decided to go up that tree instead of coming after you," said Johnny. "The scratches you got from diving into the raspberry bushes are minor compared to what the mother bear would have done to you," said Johnny. "That was pretty exciting even though it was dumb," said Sam. Looking up in the tree at the mother bear and her cubs, the boys decided to leave before she came down.

Large, dark thunder clouds were forming which indicated good fishing. For some reason, fish seem to be very active just before a rainstorm. Arriving at the hill, overlooking the lake, a beautiful scene unfolded before the boys' eyes. The lake, surrounded by tall pine trees, was like a mirror, as there wasn't even a whisper of wind. The leaves on the maple and aspen trees were motionless and silent. The one movement was the gliding of a loon, flying over the lake. There was not a sound to be heard from the birds in the forest, or from the frogs in the lake. It was eerie, but very beautiful and it seemed like time had stood still. The view looked like a picture postcard.

Looking at each other, Johnny and Sam started unloading the car. Not saying anything to each other, the boys were in awe of the silent surroundings. Johnny said, "Let's go get those fish!" The boys walked down the hill to the shore of the lake. Feeling the humidity building up, Sam said, "I think we are in for a doozy of a rainstorm." Johnny said, "I think you're right, but the fish go into a feeding frenzy before a thunderstorm. Down by the shore, somebody had formed a circle of rocks, where they had built a campfire. The boys decided against building a fire, considering the impending rain. A large, dark cloud in the distance could be seen over the top of the tall pines. Johnny said, "We have an hour before the rain gets here." With that said, fishing poles went into action, using the artificial lures as bait. After a couple of casts, Johnny got a hard strike while reeling in the lure. "Got one on the line," yelled Johnny, as he started reeling in the hard-fighting, jumping bass. After landing the fish, Johnny said, "This is the biggest bass I've ever caught." Johnny measured the large, small-mouthed bass and said, "Its twenty-two inches long and must weigh eight or nine pounds."At that same moment, Sam exclaimed, "I've got one on the line and it's a big one!" The fish jumped out of the water trying to shake the lure loose. It swam from side-to-side, making it hard for Sam to reel it in. After Sam landed his big fish, Johnny measured it and said, "Wow!" "It's bigger than mine!" "Its twenty-four inches long," said Johnny. "I'll bet it weighs at least ten pounds," said Sam.

Few fishermen fished this lake, as it was pretty remote. "We can't tell anyone about these large bass," said Johnny. The boys figured the lake would be fished out within a year, if word got out about the oversized bass. The boys filled the milk pail with the lake water and stuck their bass in it. With the dark cloud approaching nearer, Johnny got out his largest lure.

"I want to see if there is anything in this lake that will go after a lure eight inches long," said Johnny. There was an old wooden boat that had been pulled up onto shore with boards in it used for paddling. "Help me get this boat in the water," said Johnny. They put the pail with the huge bass, in the boat. After some pushing and pulling, the boys got the boat in the water; it floated and didn't appear to leak. Although a large coffee can was under the middle seat. They speculated that the coffee container would have been used to hold bait, or to bail water out of the boat. With no life preservers to wear, the boys decided to use the spare tire from the car to keep them afloat, in case the boat sank. After paddling out to deeper water, Johnny slung the large lure through the air. It made quite a splash and sent ripples along the top of the glass-smooth lake. The storm would be at the lake in about twenty to thirty minutes. "We will have to get back to shore before the storm hits," said Sam.

Sam had cast out toward the center of the lake and had gotten a strike. "I got one," said Sam and he began reeling in the fish. Johnny said, "Something is playing with my lure." Sam reeled in a nice bass and put it in the pail. All of a sudden, Johnny's line became taunt and his reel began to spin; unable to stop the reel from spinning, Johnny just held onto the rod. When the line ran out on the reel, the rod bent and the boat started to move in the direction of whatever was on the line. After pulling the boat for about fifty feet, the line went limp.

Johnny started to reel the line in, when it went taunt again. Whatever was on the end of the line had to be enormous. With the storm now getting closer, Johnny decided to cut the line and get back to shore. Then the elusive fish, full of long, sharp teeth, jumped out of the water, about fifty yards away; dancing across the water on its tail, it threw the lure from its mouth and settled back into the lake. Much to Sam and Johnny's surprise, it was over eight feet long. "What kind of fish was that," asked Johnny?" "I don't know; I've never seen anything like it," said Sam. After reeling in their lines, a cold feeling overcame the boys. In their astonishment over the giant fish, they didn't notice the leak which had developed in the bottom of the boat. The water was about two inches deep in the boat and was coming in faster than the boys could bail it out with the coffee can and pail. It became obvious that the boat was going to sink; they were in deep water and at least a hundred yards from shore. Sam said, "Well, it's a good thing we brought the car tire because we're going to need it to get to shore." Even though both boys could swim, the weight of their wet clothes and boots would make it too difficult to swim all the way to shore.

All of a sudden, it became dark, due to the approaching storm. A big bolt of lightning struck the lake and lit up the sky. "That was close," exclaimed Johnny! With the combination of the darkness, the pounding rain, and waves whipped up by the strong gusts of wind, it was hard to see anything. "We better get to shore fast before this boat sinks," said Johnny. The boys started paddling fast for shore when the giant fish came up out of the water, by the boat and lunged at Sam. Sam leaned back and the teeth of the giant fish just missed him. The giant fish landed in the boat causing it to sink. The boys grabbed the tire with one hand while paddling with the other. They went in the direction of the waves, hoping to find the shore in the blinding rain. The wind stopped and the waves subsided. Unable to see where they were going because of the heavy downpour and dim light, they became disoriented and began to wonder if they had been paddling in circles. It was hard hanging onto the tire which added to the frustration of not being able to see the shore.

Johnny felt something grab the heel of one of his boots. "Something just grabbed my boot," yelled Johnny. It was pulling hard and Johnny had to grip the tire with both hands to keep from being pulled under water. Johnny tried kicking at whatever had a hold of his boot with his other leg, but it didn't help. Whatever had a hold on his boot was pulling the boys and the tire through the water. Fearing the worst, Johnny said, "Sam, I can't hold on much longer."

Johnny was exhausted from trying to hang onto the tire with something huge pulling on his boot. After ten more minutes of struggling, Johnny said, "Sam, I can't hold on any longer and I'm letting go of the tire." Johnny's hands slipped off the tire and he fell backward into the water. Whatever had been pulling on Johnny's boot let go. Trying to regain some strength to grasp the tire, Johnny started to kick his feet. One foot hit something solid and then something slapped against his face. Then his other foot hit something solid and when he tried to stand up, he almost fell forward into the water. When he regained his balance, he found himself in chest-deep water. He was standing near the shore and the thing that hit him in the face was a cattail. Johnny hollered for Sam and was surprised that the answer came from such a short distance away. "Sam, stand up and you should be able to touch the bottom with your feet," yelled Johnny. "I can feel the bottom," said Sam. Together, through the rain and blackness, the boys pulled the spare tire to shore. With the rain still coming down hard, the boys made it up the hill to the car. After putting the spare tire in the trunk, the shelter of the car felt great. Thank goodness the car started and the warmth from the heater felt like a roaring fireplace. Too exhausted to drive and with the rain still coming down in torrents, the cold, wet boys closed their eyes and dozed.It sounded like a thousand small hammers hitting the car; the furious storm was sending hail to the now drenched area. The hail was small, but left a blanket of ice pellets almost two inches deep; it looked like winter had returned. Once the hail had passed, the rain let up a little. With lighter rain coming down, the boys decided to leave the lake and headed for home. Turning off the lake road and onto the forestry road, Johnny felt how slippery the clay road was. Even though Johnny drove as slow as possible, the car kept sliding from one side of the road to the other. Then, one side of the car went into the ditch while the other side had wheels on the road. With the big mud and snow tires on the back, Johnny was able to move the car back and forth in an effort to get all four wheels up onto the toad. By backing up a further distance, Johnny thought he could make a faster run in the ditch and cut the wheels to get back on the road. When he started driving forward the car slid sideways and lodged deeper into the ditch. The car kept sliding sideways until the passenger side of the car rested against a large tree. With the large tree against the passenger door, the car was stuck and wouldn't budge. Shining a flashlight out of the window, Sam said, "Let's get out of the car; there is a deep ravine on my side."

The boys got out of the car and saw their predicament. They had been saved by the tree from rolling the car into a fifty-foot deep ravine. Now the reality of a long walk was before them. It was thirty-five miles to the nearest occupied house. The hard rain had let up, but there was still a drizzle coming down. With a flashlight, the boys started walking down the muddy road toward home. It was tiring plodding down the dark road with clay caked on their wet boots. It was silent except for the occasional screeching of a hawk soaring above them.

Deer had come out onto the road to escape the dripping wet forest. The blowing sound that deer make to warn each other of danger could be heard close by, in the darkness. Wondering about the bear they had encountered earlier that day was on their minds. Having walked about five miles through the slushy mud and clay on the road, the boys were tired. The ditches were full of water, so they had to rest right in the middle of the road. Sam said, "Let's take a break," and plopped down right in the wet clay, on the road. Johnny agreed and sat down in the mud next to Sam. "My feet hurt," said Johnny, who had switched from his hiking boots to a pair of rubber boots that were in the car. The soft-soled rubber boots didn't provide much protection from the round gravel on the road. "I made a mistake switching to these rubber boots; I thought they would be more comfortable than those water-soaked leather hiking boots" said Johnny. "It sure would be a lot easier walking if we had some light; it's kind of scary out here," said Sam. Johnny and Sam had an uncomfortable fifteen minute back-to-back rest, in the middle of the wet, muddy road. The boys regained some of their strength and continued on their journey home.

The boys were covered in mud on their boots and also on the seats of their pants; walking was becoming harder and harder by the minute. About an hour later and a couple of miles further down the road, the moon peeked out through the cloudy, dark sky. The moon was full and lit up the road before them. It was a welcome sight to be able to see the road and where they were walking. The sky became clear with the full, bright moon and stars overhead. "We needed light and nature has provided it for us," said Johnny. The boys, in a much better mood, began singing songs, as they trudged down the long road. They split the leftover hot dogs and they tasted so good. The buns were a little soggy, but the hot dogs inside were delicious. It must have been about midnight, the boys thought, as they approached a crossroad where they had to turn and go south on a higher, less muddy road. There was more gravel which made Johnny's feet hurt worse. After a short distance down that road, they could see an abandoned hunting shack. "Let's see if we can get into that old shack and take a rest; my feet need a break," said Johnny. When they reached the shack, they could see that all the windows were broken and the door was open. Through the dim light of the moon, they could see an old bed with a mildewed mattress lying on some rusty springs. What a welcome sight, the boys thought, as they crawled onto the musty smelling mattress. Within a few minutes, they fell asleep.

The morning sun was just rising and the darkness was giving way to daylight. All of a sudden, Sam yelled, "There's something in the bed with us!" Johnny rolled over and his hand struck something sharp and painful. "Ouch!" yelled Johnny, as he rolled off the mattress. Now, wide awake, he saw what was in the bed with them. It was a big porcupine. Johnny slung his hand around and it landed on the porcupine's back. With a half dozen quills sticking out of his hand, Johnny said, "Let's get out of here!" The porcupine waddled out the door with Johnny and Sam not far behind.

Johnny's hand was in pain and he needed to get the quills out. With the sun starting to give more light, Johnny took his universal tool out of its pouch. The tool had a knife, scissors, and pliers, all in one unit. "You'll have to cut the tips of the quills off and pull them out," said Johnny to Sam. Johnny had watched his father and uncle remove porcupine quills from his dog, Butch. Johnny knew that cutting the tips off the quills would make them deflate and easier to remove. It would hurt pulling the barbed quills out of his hand, thought Johnny.

Sam, cut the tips of the barbed quills off and said, "Are you ready?" Johnny said, "Yes, yank them out." Sam grabbed the first quill with the pliers and gave it a quick yank; out came the first quill with a spurt of blood. Biting his lip, Johnny was trying not to scream out loud. It hurt and now he knew why Butch had to be wrapped in a carpet and held down while pulling out his quills. With five more to go, Johnny told Sam to go ahead and finish pulling out the quills. With each quill that came out, Johnny felt more relieved. "Thanks, Sam," said Johnny whose hand was bloody and throbbing from the ordeal.

"I feel like a doctor," said Sam, as he returned the universal tool to Johnny.

"We had better start down the road home, as we still have a long way to go," said Johnny. Along the edges of the road were blackberry bushes with large, juicy berries on them. Hungry and thirsty, the boys began feasting on the delicious, plump berries. The sun began rising and its warmth felt good to the boys, as it dried the clothes they were wearing. There was a spring bubbling out of an outcropping of rock alongside the road. The boys drank their fill of the sweet, natural spring water and washed the mud off their faces and arms. The icy-cold spring water felt refreshing on Johnny's swollen, throbbing hand where the quills had been removed. The boys felt energized, now that they had eaten all those juicy, ripe blackberries and had drunk all that pure, spring water; they continued down the drying gravel road toward home.

It was a Sunday morning and the chances of a car coming down that particular road seemed remote. Johnny said, "Sam, do you think that whatever had a hold of my boot wanted to eat me?" "It might have been trying to take a bite out of you, but it wasn't big enough to devour you," said Sam. I guess my hiking boots were too tough to be bitten through," said Johnny. "I wonder what kind of fish that was that danced across the water," asked Sam? "Sturgeons get that big, but they are not leapers," said Sam. "That fish had to have been close to three hundred pounds," said Johnny.

A slight roar was coming up behind the boys. It was a long, shiny black Cadillac with dark windows and driving very slow. Moving to the side of the road, the boys stuck out their thumbs, hoping to get a ride, after walking twenty miles. The Cadillac slowed almost to a crawl with faces staring out the windows at the boys in their muddy clothes and boots. When the boys approached the luxury car, it sped off in a cloud of dust from the now dried road. Someone was sightseeing, or lost, as the license plates were from out-of-state.

Disappointed, the boys looked at each other and then burst into uncontrollable laughter, pointing at the car going down the road. "I'll bet they thought we were wild boys who lived in these remote woods," said Johnny. "They took our picture and will tell their friends that we were half animal and half human," said Sam. The laughter made the walk seem almost bearable. Starting down a hill about a mile long, the boys heard the groaning of a truck engine hauling logs. It topped the hill behind them and was loaded with a trailer full of logs. The truck wouldn't be able to stop until it reached the bottom of the hill and would need speed to make it up the other side. The truck driver blew his horn to acknowledge the boys who waved back, knowing that the driver couldn't stop.

At the bottom of the hill were some apple trees with ripe apples on the top limbs. There were bear and deer tracks below the trees. Animals had eaten all the apples off the lower limbs, but had left the ones alone that they couldn't reach. Using a dead limb, Sam knocked some of the apples down to the ground. The apples were crisp, sweet and helped cut down on the hunger pains the boys were experiencing. After eating their fill of the delicious wild apples, the boys rested in the shade of the apple tree. Twenty-five miles had been covered and the boys were tired.

After a short rest, the boys were passed by a car going in the opposite direction. It may have been someone looking for them, but they sped past before the boys could get out onto the road. Weary, but knowing that they were less than ten miles from home, the boys got back on the road and started walking. About five miles further down the road, a pickup pulling a boat, went by in the opposite direction. Some young adults were in it headed for one of the local lakes; they waved as they passed the boys.

Tired, but happy that they were almost home, the boys decided not to accept any rides and fulfill their long trek on foot. A mile from Sam's farm, the boys were met by Sam's father, who was wondering what had happened to them. Sam explained about the car sliding off the road and into the ditch. They were offered a ride home by Sam's father, but declined and explained their reason to complete the journey on foot. Sam's father understood, but there was work to be done on the farm when he got back. After stopping at Sam's farm for some water, Johnny continued on his way home. Upon arriving at home, Johnny's mother was glad to see him and wondered where the car was. After explaining what had happened, Johnny's mother gave him some fresh baked bread with homemade cheese. "You'll have to go into the woods and tell your father what happened and he will expect you to work this afternoon," said Johnny's mother. Still tired, but feeling nourished, Johnny headed out into the woods to find his father and uncle who were sawing down trees, to send to the paper mill. Arriving at the location where the men were working, Johnny's father said, "Why didn't you come home last night?" After hearing Johnny's story about the car sliding off the road and the long walk, Johnny's father said, "We will stop work soon and go get the car."

Using the logging truck with a hydraulic hoist, they headed for the lake where the car was in the ditch. Using the hoist, Johnny's father picked the front end of the car off the ground. Moving the truck down the road, the car was pulled up onto the road. "You sure were lucky that tree was there to keep you from rolling into that deep ravine," said Johnny's father.

The ride home in the car was very enjoyable, as Johnny remembered his and Sam's experience of the long walk home. The next time, he would wait until weather conditions were better, before venturing out with the car during a storm. After supper, Johnny laid down in his comfortable bed thinking about his next adventure and fell sound asleep.

CHAPTER 5
MYSTERIOUS SWAMP CREATURES

The sky was cloudless and blue, without even a whisper of wind. The frost was still lingering in the shadows of the morning sunlight. It was a free day for Johnny; no work or school to contend with. The bright, fall colors of the leaves on the trees made the day seem even more enchanting.

Butch had gone with Johnny's father to get supplies for the farm. Johnny loved having Butch along when he went on adventures in the forest. He was a good companion on trips, as well as protection from wild animals. Without wanting to waste this great day, Johnny decided to go exploring in the deep forest. He filled his backpack with food, safety supplies, and his compass. Since Butch would not be coming along for protection, Johnny decided to take a rifle with him. Johnny said, "Mother, I'm going on a walk into the forest southeast of the farm." "Okay, just be back before dark," replied his mother. Johnny picked up the rifle, bullets, his backpack, and headed out into the cool, crisp morning. The air was pure and very refreshing. This was going to be a wonderful day! He decided to head toward Silver Mountain. No one lived in the forest beyond his farm and Johnny had never encountered another person in that part of the forest. The recent forest fire had left charred trees south of the farm, but toward the southeast, the stands of tall trees were still there.

After walking on the high ridge of a ravine, it was time to get down and cross the river. Looking for a place to cross, Johnny spotted a tree that had fallen across the river. While crossing on the fallen tree, Johnny's feet slipped out from under him. The rifle, which was slung over one shoulder by a leather strap, became wedged between two limbs during Johnny's fall. This stopped him from falling all the way down into the river below. But now, he was hanging above the cold, rushing water by one arm. With the rifle strap under one armpit, he grabbed a branch with his free hand. He pulled himself up onto the tree and continued across to the other bank. On the other side, Johnny started up the steep embankment of the ravine.

Once on top of the other ridge, a look back down the ravine revealed a spectacular, panoramic view of the beautiful fall colors. Small animals were scurrying around, preparing for the winter; they paid little attention to Johnny's presence. A flying squirrel sailed overhead from a large maple tree to the ground. Johnny was amazed at how far the squirrel could glide by extending its legs out to form a "kite-like" shape. The forest was filled with the chattering of animals and calls from birds.

Johnny heard the honking of geese overhead and looked up to see the flock flying in the familiar "V" formation; he witnessed the changing of the lead goose during flight. The lead goose would drop down from the head of the flock and would go to the end of the "V" formation, allowing another goose to take over the lead. It was rumored that certain geese were familiar with particular landmarks and would take the lead during those portions of the flight.

A very unusual sight came into view further down the ravine. Near the top of a huge elm tree, there were two different species of animals; on one of the limbs was a porcupine and in the main fork of the tree, was a black bear. They were both basking in the warm rays of the sun, and were oblivious to each other, as well as to Johnny's presence.

After a short rest at the top of the ravine, Johnny continued on his trek through the forest. The cool air smelled fresh and there was a slight rustling sound from leaves falling to the forest floor. Small trees showed evidence where deer had been rubbing the velvet off their horns. Deer have excellent hearing and can run fast, making it easy to avoid contact with humans.

Taking a reading on his compass, Johnny headed due southeast. Johnny was always on the lookout for birds-eye maple which is valuable and very scarce. The wood of the birds-eye maple has beautiful patterns created by nature. The trees sell for thousands of dollars each. The way to identify these trees was to look at the base of the tree which had protrusions called pimples. Sometimes, the trees seem to be deformed and darker than most hard-maple trees. The beautiful wood is used in the interior of expensive cars and to laminate fine furniture.

The sky was a deep blue with an occasional white, fluffy cloud floating by. A large, bald eagle was soaring high above and enjoying the warm sunlight and light breeze. The walking was easy, since the frost had killed the ferns and tall grass. The rapid pecking of a woodpecker could be heard in the distance; it sounded like someone using a jack hammer. Johnny was always amazed when he saw a tree where a woodpecker had been working. The tree was full of holes and there were wood chips scattered all around the trunk. He wondered if woodpeckers ever got headaches from the constant pecking and noise.

Johnny was headed toward the great cedar swamp which most people avoided. He had heard of strange things happening in that swamp, but he thought most stories were exaggerated, to become more interesting. The swamp was several miles long and a few miles wide. Johnny decided to venture into the swamp to see what was so mysterious about this place.

After all, he had a rifle for protection and a compass to tell him the direction in which he was traveling. Taking a compass reading, Johnny headed south into the swamp.

Cattails surrounded the swamp's edge for about twenty yards. Avoiding the deep puddles of water among the cattails, Johnny worked his way to the trees. Peering into the cedar thicket, it was quite dark with very little light coming through the dense trees. I wish Butch were with me right now, thought Johnny; with his keen sense of smell and hearing, he would have alerted Johnny to any danger. Butch was fearless and had chased a bear out of the yard at the farmhouse. Being a dog used to herding sheep, he was quick and could avoid the slower movements of a bear, while nipping at the bear's hind legs.

Moss and swamp grass grew among the dead, fallen trees. Entering the dark, damp, foreboding floor of the swamp, Johnny noticed the eerie silence and lack of birds. The absence of noise allowed Johnny to hear his own breathing. He thought he could hear his own heart beating, but it was his pulse increasing with excitement. Taking a few deep breaths, Johnny entered the swamp. Deer had made trails through the dense trees and tall stands of swamp grass. Swamp grass was abundant in the swamp and grew to be heights of five to six feet. Other animals such as rabbits, foxes, coyotes, and wolves used the swamp for protection from the elements.

Johnny saw evidence of these animals by tracks in the dark, wet soil of the swamp floor. Droppings from the animals also identified which animals had been through the area. One track that concerned Johnny was a large cat track; that of a mountain lion. Bobcats were common in the area, mountain lions were not.

Crossing over a fallen tree, Johnny reached up to get a hand hold. Something moved under his hand and he jerked it away from the tree. His hand had landed on a long snake. Johnny's whole body shook and a cold shiver went up his spine, as the long, dark snake slithered off the log and disappeared into the thick swamp grass. The snake was about six feet long and as big around as Johnny's calf; it appeared to be a pine snake. While not poisonous, it was still intimidating because of its size. The snake had been as startled as Johnny and was just trying to escape the encounter.

After regaining his composure, Johnny continued along the deer trail. Just ahead, sunlight was shining through the tall, thick growth of cedars. A small meadow came into view, as Johnny approached the sunlight. Entering the meadow, Johnny felt the warmth of the sun overhead. Feeling relieved to be out of the creepy swamp and back into daylight, Johnny decided to stop and have his lunch. Johnny discovered a spring bubbling clear, cold water, out of the ground, in the meadow. He washed his face and hands with the cold water which was very refreshing. The springs in the area produced excellent, good-tasting water and Johnny drank his fill. The summer sausage sandwiches tasted good with the hot coffee he made. The warm sun made Johnny sleepy and he decided to close his eyes for a few minutes and take a little nap.

The overhead screech of a hawk awakened Johnny from his deep slumber. He wondered how long he had been napping as he checked his watch. Two hours had gone by and the sun had disappeared from the sky. Clouds had replaced the clear, blue sky and there was a chill in the air. A snort from across the meadow caught Johnny's attention. It was the unmistakable sound of a male deer.

Johnny's eyes grew big at the sight across the meadow. He was staring at the largest whitetail buck he had ever seen. Could this be Old Pete, the elusive buck that hunters had tried to get in their gun sights for as many years as Johnny could remember? He had been seen by a few people and never during hunting season. As hard as they looked for him, the hunters sometimes found the large hoof prints he left behind to tease them.

The hair on his back was dark with some gray showing through. He stood very erect and proud with his massive pair of antlers. He was much taller and wider than a normal mature buck. His broad chest, large, thick neck, and strong, large legs showed the power of this deer. He appeared to weigh twice as much as the average buck. His hooves were almost as big as those of a dairy cow.

Johnny had seen his tracks before, on other adventures, but never the actual deer. Almost paralyzed by the awesome sight, Johnny watched the huge deer start to cross the meadow toward him. Without knowing the intentions of the massive deer, Johnny readied his rifle. The deer walked in the direction where Johnny was sitting with his back against a tree. The deer was not charging, but was curious at Johnny's presence in the swamp. The oversized deer walked close to Johnny, sniffing to get his scent. He stopped about ten yards from Johnny and pawed the ground. Johnny had seen other bucks paw the ground before charging.

Johnny was staring into the eyes of the huge deer and it was staring back. Johnny had an apple in his backpack and wondered if the buck would come close enough to take it. Johnny took the apple out of his backpack and tossed it toward the deer. The deer sniffed the air and could smell the aroma of the apple. With one hand on his rifle, Johnny watched as the deer came closer. The buck lowered his head with the massive set of antlers and approached Johnny. Johnny wasn't sure he was going to charge, or would take the apple. The buck stopped about ten feet from Johnny and stared at him. Not sensing danger from Johnny, the buck approached him. Johnny couldn't believe what just happened and took his finger off the trigger of his rifle. The buck raised his head and trotted off through the tall swamp grass. Johnny would tell Sam of this encounter but no one else. The huge buck's hiding place would be known and kept a secret by Johnny and Sam.

A chill came over Johnny, as he noticed a drop in the temperature. Johnny put on his backpack, took a compass reading, and started walking out of the swamp. Snowflakes were now fluttering down from the grey sky. It would be getting dark in two or three hours. The swamp was darker with the snow coming down and the clouds had shut off the sunlight. Trails don't look the same when you walk them in the opposite direction, so Johnny checked his compass often. After walking for about an hour, Johnny saw what appeared to be the edge of the swamp. When he got to the opening, he realized that he had walked in a circle. He was back in the same meadow he had left an hour earlier. Johnny's compass seemed to work okay, but was misdirected by something in the swamp. Johnny started to think about the strange things that people said had happened in the swamp. The snow was coming down much heavier and it was getting darker. Johnny decided to start gathering wood for a fire and prepare to spend the night in the swamp. It would be easier to find his way out tomorrow in the daylight. Johnny knew his parents would be worried about him with the heavy snow falling. They also knew he could survive in these situations. He had been taught not to venture into the unknown, if he were in a safe place. He didn't want to risk trying to go back through the cedar swamp at night. The dense cedar trees provided an overhead shelter from the snow and dry limbs would be used to build a fire. Finding a good spot, under a clump of close growing cedar trees, Johnny started gathering dry moss and limbs to build a fire. Having gathered enough wood for the night, Johnny built a roaring fire that would last through most of the night. Once the fire was burning, Johnny laid cedar boughs with their fernlike soft texture, on the ground, to make a soft bed for himself.

Johnny's backpack contained emergency provisions for an unexpected situation such as this. A large tin cup, used for boiling water, was filled with the spring water to make hot coffee. Eating some homemade cookies with the hot coffee had a calming effect. While lying down by the warm, crackling fire, Johnny wondered what animals lived in the swamp.

He didn't have to wait long before he heard the yipping of coyotes. After putting more wood on the fire, Johnny dozed off and was awakened a short time later by the howl of a wolf. The howl was close, so Johnny grabbed his rifle and fired a shot in the air. The howl occurred again but this time it sounded further away. Johnny felt uneasy; he sat up, wide awake. He stared into the fire, glancing at the strange looking shadows and shapes made by the swamp grass. It felt as though someone or something was watching him, even though he didn't see or hear anything. The heat from the fire comforted him and Johnny started to feel sleepy again. Nearby, an ear-piercing scream brought him out of his slumber and up onto his feet. He had never heard anything like that in his life. It was similar to a mountain lion, but had a lower pitch. Now, wide awake with his adrenalin flowing, Johnny sat upright with his back against a tree, clutching his rifle for protection. Unable to sleep anymore for the rest of the night, he added the rest of the wood to the fire to give out more light to the surrounding area. Every now and then, Johnny could hear something cracking brush in the swamp.   What was it that made the eerie scream, thought Johnny? A mountain lion would have had a higher pitched scream, but would have moved through the forest without making any noise. Bears would make noise going through the brush but they didn't scream. It was going to be a long night, as Johnny decided he had better stay awake until daylight.

Toward morning, Johnny kept dozing as he tried to stay awake. The fire was dying down when Johnny was awakened by the low pitched scream again. It was close this time and it made shivers go up and down his spine. Johnny stood up and looked around at the dark, strange shadows of the swamp. Something was moving in the tall swamp grass to his left. Johnny thought he could hear it breathing. He leveled his rifle in the direction of the moving grass and cocked the trigger. Whatever was in the grass was making low growling noises. Johnny saw a pair of eyes looking at him through the swamp grass, but couldn't make out a shape of the animal. There was just enough light from the fire to make the eyes shine in the dark. Then the eyes disappeared and there was no sound coming from the tall, swamp grass. A clump of snow plopped down from a tree, onto the fire, almost putting it out. It was still dark. The animal let out a loud, blood-curdling scream and charged in the direction of Johnny. Johnny fired a shot from his rifle into the air, hoping to scare it. The animal stopped short of coming into the opening of the meadow, staying hidden behind the tall swamp grass. Johnny could hear it growling and breaking brush, as it moved around, out of his sight. Johnny didn't hear that animal anymore, but it could still be lurking in the shadows of the night.

The snow had stopped falling and a few breaks in the clouds showed light from a full moon. Johnny kept the fire burning until daylight and then put it out. With the sun coming up, Johnny knew which was east and wouldn't use his compass. In the daylight, Johnny checked the area behind the swamp grass and saw tracks of a huge animal. The tracks were larger than bear tracks and the animal had been walking on two legs, which would not have been normal for a bear. Johnny was very puzzled by this. What could it have been, he thought?

After thirty minutes of walking, the sky clouded up and it began to rain. Johnny figured he would be out of the swamp in forty-five minutes. Over an hour went by and Johnny wasn't out of the swamp. He couldn't trust his compass and the sun had disappeared when the rain started to come down. Johnny thought, I'm lost, but I can follow my tracks back to the meadow and wait for the sky to clear. The problem was that the rain was melting the snow and the tracks were disappearing. Soon Johnny couldn't see any more tracks. He was now lost in the swamp. He looked for moss that grows on the north side of trees; but in the swamp, moss grew on all sides of the trees. Johnny figured that if he walked in a straight line using three landmarks, he would come out of the swamp somewhere. After two more hours of walking, Johnny saw cattails; he sighed with relief. He could now get out of the swamp and then use his compass to get back home. Johnny made his way through the cattails to the other bank. There was a small lake on the other shore. It was a strange looking lake; there was moss hanging down from the trees surrounding the lake.

Johnny sat down on the bank of the lake and noticed that he was quite warm. While sitting, Johnny thought he saw a stone statue through the trees. He got up and started walking toward it. Sure enough, it was a carved statue of stone covered with vines. The statue was about ten feet tall; the figure looked like a human. The eyes were enormous; so was the mouth with canine looking teeth. There were horns coming out of each side of the head. This was weird, thought Johnny. Who had made this statue?

There was a cave near the statue. Johnny could hear noises, in the woods, on the other side of the lake. Johnny ran to the cave entrance for protection. He peered out to see what was making those noises. There were several tall, dark figures moving through the shadows. The water on the other side of the lake exploded; a twenty-foot long crocodile rushed through the cattails, in the direction of the tall, dark figures. A lot of high-pitched screams came from the other side of the lake. Johnny looked back in the cave for a place to hide, but it was too dark to see anything. Johnny looked down on the floor of the cave and saw two human skulls.

The crocodile didn't come back to the lake; Johnny couldn't see, or hear the dark figures anymore. Crocodiles don't live up north and couldn't survive the winters, thought Johnny. However, if the water of the lake was warm and heated by an underground source, jungle creatures could survive. Johnny made a quick dash to the edge of the lake; indeed, the water was warm. What other creatures could be lurking in this area of the swamp, thought Johnny? It didn't take long for Johnny to find out. Just as he rose from touching the lake water, a large python was swimming in his direction. Not wanting to show his presence at the lake, Johnny took off running toward the cattails that he came through earlier. Once through the cattails, Johnny was back near the cedar swamp. Nobody was going to believe what Johnny saw; he decided not to tell anyone about the warm lake, the crocodile, the statue, the snake, the skulls, or even the dark figures. Johnny decided to follow the cattails in the opposite direction from the lake. After an hour, the cattails disappeared and it was back into the cedar swamp again.

It was in the afternoon and Johnny was lost; the compass wouldn't work. The rain had stopped, but the sky was cloudy. Not knowing which way to go, Johnny sat down on a log to take a break. Then Johnny heard a familiar sound; it was a flock of geese. He got to an open spot and could see the flying "V" formation of the flock. He knew which way to go, as the geese were going south for the winter. Johnny kept three points in a straight line; in two hours Johnny was at the edge of the swamp where he had started his journey.

He knew his parents would be worried and would start looking for him. Reaching the edge of the swamp, Johnny crossed through the cattails, trying not to step in the water holes. He heard three rifle shots after he passed through the cat tails. It was Johnny's father signaling the direction of home. Johnny fired three rifle shots to let him know that he had heard him. The snow was about a foot deep, making walking a little slow. Johnny headed for the hill which led to the river. After a slow, slippery walk down the hill, he reached the river. Being cautious, Johnny crossed back over the river on the fallen tree without any mishaps. Several deer were further down the river, getting a drink of water. They snorted, flashed their white tails, and trotted off into the woods.

Arriving at the farm, Johnny was greeted with good hearted kidding about not knowing how to read a compass. Relief could be seen in the faces of Johnny's parents, knowing that he was safe. A couple of uncles and some neighbors had come over to form a search party. After the ribbing was over, everyone went into the house for coffee and hot, fresh baked cinnamon rolls. They all sat around the large, wooden kitchen table and began explaining to Johnny why his compass didn't work in the swamp; it was due to deposits of iron in the area, which affected compass readings. Everyone agreed that Johnny made the right decision to stay overnight in the swamp instead of trying to make it out of there in the dark. They also commended Johnny for building an extra large fire for both warmth and protection.

When Johnny told everyone about the screams and that some large animal had been roaming around the campfire, a very puzzled look came over their faces. One of Johnny's uncles said it was a bear and it just sounded like it screamed. Johnny had heard bears make different sounds, but not like the ones he had heard last night. Johnny said, "It walked on two legs with footprints much larger than a bear." The puzzled look returned to everyone's' faces.

One of the neighbors said, "People have been known to go into that swamp and have never come out. There has been a legend about large, hairy men living in there. Search parties have gone there looking for missing people, but no signs of them have ever been found." "The swamp is hard to search because it is too dense with cedar trees and swamp grass," said Johnny's uncle. "It is rumored that Sasquatches live in there," said a neighbor. No one has ever seen one, so it's a rumor," said Johnny's uncle. There have been many mysteries connected with that swamp but so far, none have been solved. As the adults talked on and on, speculating as to what could have screamed in the swamp, Johnny was already planning his next adventure.

CHAPTER 6
RATTLESNAKE RITUAL

With the long, cold winter approaching, Johnny's father was faced with very little work. He decided that everyone would move to New Mexico where he had been offered a short-term contract job, at a new potash mine. When it was over, they would return to the farm. This would be the second time Johnny had been uprooted from his hometown school and the country farm, to go to New Mexico. The first time was in grade school, several years earlier where Johnny attended Hispanic schools. Many of the kids in Johnny's classes were older and bigger; they had to adjust to the classes that were taught in English, as English was their second language. Most of the students had been held back one year or more, to allow for their adjustment to learning in the English language. Ninety-eight percent of the students in the school were of Hispanic descent and spoke Spanish at home. The time Johnny heard English spoken during the school day was in the classroom. Before school, during recess, and after school, Spanish was spoken among the regular students.

Johnny was blond, blue-eyed, and fair-skinned; he stood out as being new to the school. He was ignored by the local kids during recess for the first few days. The other student in the class that was not Hispanic was a skinny, shy boy named Jimmy. He told Johnny that he was afraid of the Latino boys because they called him names and made fun of him every chance they got.

During one particular recess, a few days later, the local boys had circled around Jimmy, calling him names and pushing him to the ground. Every time he tried to get up, the local boys slammed him back down. Not used to seeing this type of behavior, Johnny pushed his way into the middle of the circle to defend his new friend, Jimmy. Now, the bullies turned their attention to Johnny. They started calling him mean-sounding names in Spanish, sneering at him, and pushed him to the ground. Unlike Jimmy, Johnny got up and charged the boy who pushed him, knocking him to the ground. Every time Johnny was thrown to the ground, he got up and fought right back. Although younger and smaller than the other boys, Johnny was strong from working in the woods and doing farm chores. Pretty soon, the bullies made the circle larger, not wanting to be charged by fierce and fearless Johnny. Bruised and with a bloody nose, Johnny was not about to give up. All of a sudden, an older boy made his way through to the circle and walked over to where Johnny was standing. He said something in Spanish and the circle of bullies left the scene. He told Johnny, in English, that because he had stood up to the group and had shown no fear, he would not be picked on anymore; they were impressed with his bravery and he had won their respect. At the same time, Johnny was invited to participate in the baseball and football games played during recess and after school. From that point on, Johnny's time at the new school proved to be a rewarding experience and he made several life-long friendships.

On his second trip to New Mexico, Johnny would be going to a brand new school. Although the facilities at the new school were state of the art, one problem remained. The problem was gang fights which occurred during the lunch hour and after school. Several police squad cars showed up each day, at the school campus, to ensure the peace. The gangs consisted of the locals on one side and any newcomers on the other. Anyone who walked too close to the gang members and was a nonmember would be attacked. Recognizing several old friends from his earlier time in New Mexico, Johnny walked over to them and wasn't attacked. The local gang members were astonished! Johnny asked his old friends what the problem was. The Hispanic boys told him that the newcomers were regarded by the gang as poor and stupid. Johnny thought the idea of "stupid" was a misconception. The language barrier was the real problem. For the Hispanics, English was required to be spoken during classroom hours. The rest of the time, they spoke in their native language. Trying to learn, study, and test in English was difficult.

The leader of the local gang was the big student who had accepted Johnny when he had attended the local elementary school a few years earlier. Johnny told him that he would talk to the leader of the non-Hispanic gang to see if their differences could be resolved. When Johnny approached the leader of the non-Hispanic gang, he asked Johnny why he hadn't been attacked. Johnny told him that he had gone to school a few years ago with many of the other gang members and that several were his friends. With everyone watching, Johnny brought the two gang leaders together to try and work out their differences. The gang leaders agreed not to attack each other at school anymore and to work on a solution.

During Johnny's time at the school, differences began working out better each day. Gang members from both sides began to participate on sports teams together and in harmony. Also, the English speaking boys began tutoring the non-English speaking students, after school and on weekends. As a result, the Hispanic students began scoring higher on their tests because of this extra kindness and consideration from their former enemies, thus raising their self-esteem. They began going over to each other's homes to study and started to see and appreciate the differences in cultural backgrounds between them. They began to meet each other's families, be invited to each other's birthday parties, and started eating each other's ethnic foods. After a while, each side saw that there was very little difference in people and families in general, no matter what language they spoke. They found that they were able to communicate without speaking in the same language to each other. The gestures of appreciation and smiles on their faces could be understood in any culture without a common language ever needing to be spoken. This began to diffuse a lot of the old hostility that had built between the different cultures; as time went on, the gangs disappeared.

The Pecos River ran through the edge of town and was the best place to go fishing in the area. The river was full of schools of a fish called Shad that were two to five pounds in weight. In the deep pools of water and under the river banks, there were catfish of enormous size. The mouths were so big that the locals would stick them over the tops of fence posts.

A dam on the river provided the area residents with a great free swimming area. The multi-leveled diving platform gave spectators a view of some of the most spectacular diving events to be seen anywhere. Divers would do spins forward and backward; some with twists while flying through the air. Then they would cut into the water like a knife, without making a splash. During the hot summer days, the beach would be filled with people. The sun was so hot that most everyone used large beach umbrellas for shade. The sand would get very hot and without sandals, a hurried run across the sand was necessary. Johnny and his friends never wore sandals and always had to race across the burning sand to the cool water. After swimming for a while, Johnny and his friends would go to the park and cook hot dogs on the stationary grills provided.

The park had many large trees, so sitting in the shade with the warm breeze felt nice on their skin. During the hot days when the temperature was over one hundred degrees, the roads were closed. The black tar from the blacktop would get hot enough to drain off the road into the ditches. Most people walked to the park or took bicycles down the sidewalks on these sweltering days.

During the summer, Johnny was on a baseball team, in the Babe Ruth League. Johnny played all positions except catcher and first base. The games were very competitive and large crowds were on hand for each game. The league was sponsored by the local mines and everything provided to the team was generous and first class.

The town had a semi-pro baseball team that was always in first place in the league, or close to it. Games were very exciting, as many of the players were competing for a chance to play in the Major Leagues. One player, on an opposing team, hit seventy home runs in one season. He was a large man who would remind you of Babe Ruth and both were left-handed batters.

Due to the sweltering heat of the day, the games were played at night. The lighted field looked great at night, sometimes with the moon glowing and always with a sky full of twinkling stars. Sometimes, a shooting star would streak across the sky, causing a murmur among the spectators. A lightning storm could be seen in the distance, even though the weather was perfect for the local game. Because the land was flat, objects such as lightning and the lights of towns could be seen for distances exceeding thirty miles.

The desert, while brown and dry most of the year, comes alive with beautiful flowers after a rain. Johnny and his friends would make excursions out into the desert, looking for caves to explore. Backpacks loaded with food and survival gear were always prepared for the trips. Included was a snake bite kit, as rattlesnakes and copperheads were always present. Scorpions also seemed to be under every overturned rock.

In the distance, was a large outcropping of rock, appearing to rise one hundred feet from ground level. There should be caves in that area, so the boys headed for that rise in the distance. Extra water had been carried on the bikes, but had been left behind, due to the weight. Full canteens were taken along with the backpacks. The bikes were left at the edge of the desert, as they would be hard to ride through the loose sand. The rocky rise appeared to be about one or two miles in the distance. It was warm and sunny, but would get hotter later in the day.

The boys walked at a fast pace, as they were excited about the possibilities of what might be found in the caves. After about an hour, the rocky ridges didn't seem to be getting any closer. Taking a break with a little water from the canteens, the boys continued on their adventure. After two more hours of walking, the high rocks appeared much higher and further away than they had thought; if they continued on, they would have to stay overnight. They decided to continue on, spend the night, and return home the next day. A large rattlesnake made itself known by shaking its rattles, as it peered out from the overhang of a large boulder. As they neared the rocky foothills of the outcropping, it was about noon. The heat from the sun was getting hot. They rested in the shade of a mesquite tree, to plan the next step of their exploration. There was a cave about fifty feet up the sheer wall of the outcropping rocks, which was about three hundred feet high. They decided to walk around the outcropping to try and find a more accessible cave. Sure enough, there was a cave entrance just around the corner from where the boys had rested. The entrance was large and on the base of the outcropping. With flashlights and machetes, the boys entered the cave. The natural light from outside shined into the cave for the first fifty feet, then the darkness began. An eerie silence was noticed, as they started exploring the cave. The coolness felt refreshing, compared to the scorching heat outside. The cave appeared to have been used at one time by someone, as there was evidence of old campfires in different spots.

They continued on into the cave, looking out for snakes and other creatures along the way. Twenty minutes or so had elapsed and nothing interesting had been discovered. Shining a light up ahead, they could see that the cave split into two tunnels. They decided to stick together and explore one tunnel at a time; they chose to explore the tunnel to the right first. The boys had just begun their trek into the right tunnel when they heard a loud scream which made their blood run cold. Out of the other tunnel came a mountain lion that stopped to glare at them. With their lights shining on him, the boys yelled and beat their machetes on the tunnel walls. They managed to deter the lion from coming toward them. The lion screamed again and took off, loping toward the entrance of the cave. A little shaken, they congratulated each other on their ability to scare off such a formidable creature as a mountain lion. The boys figured the mountain lion was using the cave as his den and would stay away while they were there.

After another five minutes of walking, they came to a large room. It was hard to tell how big the room was. Just using flashlights, the boys guessed it to be at least one hundred feet wide and maybe two hundred feet long with a high ceiling. There appeared to be many objects made out of stone, some round, some square, some triangular and others rectangular.

What an odd assortment of objects, some small while others were quite large. In the center of the room was a circular area about two feet lower than the surrounding floor. The boys wondered if this could have been a place where ancient rituals had been held. There no bones anywhere that they could see, but a constant hum could be heard beneath the floor, in the center of the room. It sounded like the buzzing of a den of rattlesnakes shaking their tails. Some of the objects in the cave had rock covers on them. Some of the covers had been removed, maybe by someone who had found the cave and was looking for treasure. Shining their flashlights down into one of the round, uncovered objects, they saw the skeletons of rattlesnakes, complete with their rattles still intact. The boys had heard stories about a tribe of Indians who had lived centuries ago, in this area, who had worshiped rattlesnakes. The boys wondered if this cave could have been one of their ceremonial places.

The boys were curious as to what was in the larger square, triangular objects. They tried to slide the cover off one of them, but it was way too heavy to move; as hard as they all tried, in unison, they couldn't budge it. It looked like someone had tried to get into one of the boxes using a pry bar, but gave up because it was too difficult. A hydraulic jack would be needed to move the covers off the boxes and the boys decided they would come back another time with the proper equipment. Excitement was high, as they thought about the possibilities of uncovering treasure, or at least an historical find.

The humming in the center of the room was getting louder and the boys became concerned. They decided to leave the cave and come back at a later date with more lights and a hydraulic jack. They agreed to keep this place a secret, until they discovered the use of this room, or the finding of a great treasure. Laughing and joking about how important they were going to be, the boys started out of the cave.

In their excitement, the boys lost track of time. When they got to the entrance of the cave, the sun was starting to set. They had decided earlier that they would spend the night by the high rock formation. Walking through the desert at night could be dangerous. Snakes would be out hunting for food and would be hard to see at night. The boys gathered some dry wood near the cave entrance and started a fire for light and warmth against the cooling desert air. Settled around the warm fire and with a full moon starting to show through the clouds, they started to eat the food they had brought in their back packs. They felt safe and cozy around the fire, as they exchanged stories, laughed and joked about their adventure. It had been a long day and after eating their dinner near the warm fire, everyone fell asleep.

Johnny awoke as he felt something crawling up his arm. In the dimming light of the fire he could see a black scorpion making its way up to his chest. Not wanting to get stung, Johnny laid still, moving his eyes, to watch the scorpion. The scorpion crawled up onto Johnny's shoulder and headed for his neck. He was lingering, as if he would settle in the warmth of Johnny's neck. What seemed like an eternity, the scorpion decided to continue moving and crawled up Johnny's cheek. Approaching his nose, the scorpion crawled up onto Johnny's forehead. Then Johnny could no longer feel the scorpion on him. Ten more minutes went by and Johnny figured the scorpion had gone on his way. With a burst of energy, Johnny sprang to his feet swatting his head and shoulders with his hat. Thank goodness the scorpion was no longer on him and he let out a loud whoop. This startled the others and they jumped up to see what was wrong. After explaining his experience with the scorpion, no one got any more sleep.

Johnny got up to add some more wood to the fire. As he turned around, he was confronted by a stern looking Indian, on a horse. Petrified by what he saw, he looked around and there were more Indians on horseback. Speechless, he looked up at the big Indian who was scowling at him. Hearing Johnny talking to someone, the other boys came up behind him. Astonished at the presence of real Indians, the boys looked at each other without uttering a word. The big Indian spoke in a loud and stern voice, "What are you doing here?" All the boys tried to answer at the same time causing confusion. The Indian pointed to Johnny and said, "You tell me why you are here." Johnny said in a strong voice, "We are here exploring caves." The Indian replied, "This is an Indian Reservation and you must ask permission to enter this area."

"Did you find the big room in the cave," asked the Indian? Johnny said, "Yes, and it was full of large stone boxes." The Indian peered at the boys and said, "This cave holds the big room and is used for ceremonies. You were very lucky to have escaped with your lives." We have come here, as we do each evening, to feed the snakes that are part of our culture." Johnny thought about the humming noise in the center of the big room; it must have been coming from the rattlesnakes. The leader of the Indians said, "You boys come with us into the cave and we will show you why you should never again attempt to enter this cave." Following the Indians into the cave, the boys were apprehensive about what they were going to see. Using torches, the Indians led the way pulling large wooden boxes on wheels behind them. Johnny could hear noises coming from the boxes, so he knew that there was something alive in them. The torches the Indians were carrying gave off much more light than the flashlights the boys had used earlier.

Along the walls, there were hieroglyphics of Indians and some very large snakes. The boys had not noticed these same hieroglyphics earlier, because they had been focused on the floor of the cave and not the walls. Upon reaching the large room, the Indians lit more torches and the whole room could be seen. Along with the stone boxes were statues of snakes and more paintings on the walls. Once it was lighter, the boys were in awe of the majesty of the room. The Indians opened one of the long, rectangular boxes with apparent ease. They took wooden polls from the box which was about six feet long. With the poles, they went to the edges of the circular depression in the center of the room. With five Indians on each side of the pit, they then stuck the poles into holes about a foot deep; as they pulled on the poles the floor in the center of the pit began to open. Once the floor of the pit had opened, the humming sound was very loud.

With the light of the torches shining down into the pit, the scary sight of thousands of rattlesnakes could be seen. The Indians carried the boys over to the edge of the pit. The big Indian said, "My brave brothers want to throw you boys into the pit of rattlesnakes. They think it would be a good sacrifice; I told them, if you boys would promise to keep this cave a secret, I would let you go. There would be very bad luck for you boys if you made the promise then broke it. "I'm asking you boys for your solemn oath to keep this secret, or we will throw you to the snakes." The boys, wide-eyed and looking down at the snakes, swore an oath to keep this place a secret and never enter the cave again. The Indians pulled the boys back from the edge of the pit and lined them up against the wall. One Indian was standing in front of the boys, holding a large rattlesnake. The big Indian said, "You boys swore an oath to keep this place a secret. Each of you will have to hold the snake; if your word is not truthful, the rattlesnake will strike you. If you are struck, you will be thrown into the pit. If you mean what you said, the snake will not strike you." Johnny was the first to take the snake; it was heavy and Johnny almost dropped it. The snake didn't strike Johnny, so the Indian took it back. Each boy was given the rattlesnake and none were struck. The big Indian said, "I believe you boys. Now, we have to feed the snakes.

The wooden boxes were brought to the pit and opened. They were full of rats and mice that were dumped into the pit as food for the snakes. After moving the boxes away from the pit, the Indians once more pulled on the poles and the floor closed. The big Indian moved the boys to the back of the room. "You must stay here. Don't move and be silent," said the big Indian. The other Indians then moved the poles to the front of the pit and inserted them into different holes. By pulling on the poles, an opening about a foot and a half wide appeared, in the front of the pit. All the Indians, including the big Indian gathered in the center of the pit. Kneeling on their knees, heads bowed and hands clasped together, they began to chant. Soon, a huge rattlesnake appeared and came out of the opening; then another came out. With their hearts pounding and their eyes very wide, the boys witnessed something never seen by anyone outside of the tribe. The huge rattlers looked to be fifteen feet in length. The snakes circled around the Indians flicking their tongues. After about ten minutes, the snakes retreated back into the hole from where they had come. The Indians carried large wooden boxes, with what appeared to be larger rodents to the front of the pit. Using the poles to close the opening to the pit, the Indians then moved a stone above the pit. Into this opening were dumped the larger rodents and the stone was then replaced. The boys, who were in an almost petrified state of shock, were approached by the big Indian. "You have witnessed the feeding of the snakes. Now you know that this cave is a sacred place and you should never again enter it," said the Indian. "No one outside of the Indian tribe is allowed to see a ceremony, but the feeding of the snakes is not considered a ceremony. That is why we allowed you to witness this act. There are several stone boxes in this room which rattlesnakes use as their homes. You were lucky that you didn't disturb them, since the boxes all have holes in them. Those snakes travel on the cave floors and go out into the desert to hunt for food. You were lucky not to have run into them on your way into the cave," said the Indian. Putting out the torches in the cave and dragging the wooden boxes behind them, the Indians left the cave. The boys, still bewildered by what they had just seen, followed the Indians out of the cave. The sun had come up while the boys were inside the cave. Once outside, it took some time getting used to the bright sunlight. Now, the long walk back to the bikes was ahead.

The boys didn't have much water left in their canteens. The big Indian said, "If you boys promise to keep this place a secret, we will give you a ride back to the road." Once the boys promised to keep this place a secret, the large Indian gave each of them a rattle from a rattlesnake; he said they were honorary members of their tribe. The Indians helped the boys up onto the backs of their horses. What would have taken them hours to walk, in the hot sun, they were back to their bikes in less than thirty minutes.

Upon arriving at the place where they had left their bikes, the boys thanked the Indians for the ride. Without looking back, the Indians rode out into the desert. The boys drank some of the water they had left with their bikes. They thought it was strange that the Indian they heard speak was the big Indian. They did hear the chanting in the cave; other than that, the other Indians remained silent. Congratulating each other on their adventure, the boys started back to town on their bikes. It was about fifteen miles back to town, but with a slight breeze at their backs. About half way back to town, a sheriff's car met the boys and called them over. Since the boys hadn't shown up last night, the parents were organizing a search party to look for them. No one had told their parents that they might be staying overnight, or in which direction they were going. The sheriff called his office on his two-way radio to say that he had found the missing boys, that they were okay, and on their way back home. When asked by their parents why they had stayed overnight in the desert, the boys said they had lost track of time and thought it would be safer to stay by a campfire rather than walking in the desert late in the evening. The boys were reminded that if they went out again exploring, they should tell someone where they were going and that an overnight stay might be possible. The boys agreed with their parents and promised to do as they were asked the next time. The boys kept their word to the Indians and never revealed the secret of the sacred rattlesnake cave.

After the boys' excursion into the desert, Johnny's father completed his assignment with the mining company and they moved back to Upper Michigan.

CHAPTER 7
SUMMER ROMANCE

The last of the hay making season was in full bloom. Johnny and one of his brothers helped the neighbor farmer, Mr. Knudsen with his hay storage for the winter. The grass in the field had been cut and raked into rows to dry. After a few days, the hay was dry and ready to be put in the hay loft of the barn. This hay would feed the cattle and horses throughout the long winter. Once the hay was dry, it was time to gather it and bring it into the barn. The hay was gathered with a hay rake, mounted on the front of a pickup truck. The pickup truck would drive down the rows of hay, scooping up a pile ten feet high. It would then push the loose hay to the barn where it would be hoisted up on ropes. When a bundle reached a rail, mounted underneath the roof of the barn, it would slide into the barn through a large open door. The bundle of hay would be pulled along the rail to a spot where it needed to be dropped. Someone outside the barn held a trip rope, attached to the ropes holding the bundle of hay. This process was continued until all the hay was gathered from the fields. Sometimes, the hay would fall from the rail, in the wrong place. This would happen if the trip rope got tangled up with the carriage. The hay dropped from the top of the barn rail would fall and land in a clump, as it hit the hay below. Two people worked in the hay loft spreading the hay. Using pitch forks with curved tangs, they would pull the hay toward the walls of the hay loft, keeping the hay at an even level.

Johnny was working in the hay loft when a bundle of hay came through the opening. The people spreading the hay would stand against the walls when the hay was dropped from the rail at the top of the barn. When the hay bundle was in the right position, the spreaders would yell, "Trip the bundle," and the hay would fall into the designated area. Johnny was in the center of the hay loft, spreading hay, when a huge bundle came through the opening. When the bundle passed over him, the trip rope got tangled in the carriage, releasing the hay. The whole bundle fell on top of him, covering him with ten feet of hay. It was hard to move under several hundred pounds of hay. Struggling against the loose hay was exhausting. He could hear Jack, the other hay spreader hollering, "Are you okay?" Johnny cried out in a weak, muffled voice, "Yes, I'm here." Jack was pulling hay off the bundle with his pitch fork. Not wanting to stick Johnny with the long, sharp tangs of the pitchfork, Jack kept calling, "Where are you?" Almost unable to get any air, Johnny couldn't answer loud enough to be heard. Johnny was just about to pass out from lack of oxygen, when he felt a sharp pain near his ankle. The tangs of Jack's pitchfork had pierced Johnny's boot, sticking him in the ankle. The pain was so intense that it gave Johnny new energy, as he shouted, "Ouch!"

Jack found Johnny and pulled him out from under the hay. With a great sigh of relief, Jack said, "Sorry I stabbed you; we had better get you to the house, to stop the bleeding." With Jack's help, Johnny hobbled to the house. Mrs. Knudsen, the farmer's wife, removed his boot which was full of blood. She put alcohol on a white cloth and cleansed his foot. She crushed some ice with a hammer, wrapped it in another cloth, and pressed it over the punctures; after about five minutes, the bleeding stopped. She bandaged the wounds with sterile gauze and a stinky ointment. She then proceeded to wipe the blood from inside Johnny's boot, put a clean sock over the bandaged ankle and said, "You need to get a tetanus shot."

There's a veterinarian about two miles down the road and he could give you the shot," said Mrs. Knudsen.

Arriving at Dr. Penegor's house, Mrs. Knudsen explained what had happened. Johnny was in too much pain to walk, so Dr. Penegor came over to the pickup where Johnny was sitting. He had one hand behind his back, as he approached. "Have you ever had a tetanus shot," he asked?" "No, Sir," said Johnny. "Well, this might sting a little," as he produced a syringe with a six-inch needle from behind his back. The wide-eyed, bewildered look on Johnny's face, as he looked at the long needle, made Dr. Penegor burst out with laughter. "This big needle is what I use on horses and cows," said Dr. Penegor, smiling. "You just get a little needle, young man," he said. The shot was almost painless, compared to the pitch fork piercing his ankle, thought Johnny. "Expect a little fever tonight, but other than that, you will be fine in a day or two," said the tall veterinarian.

Without saying anything, Mrs. Knudsen stopped at another farm on the way home. When the lady of the house, Mrs. Sawyer, came out, she was accompanied by a very pretty girl with intriguing green eyes. "This is Sandy," said Mrs. Knudsen, as she introduced her to Johnny. "Nice to meet you," said Sandy to Johnny. "Hi," replied Johnny, as the girl got into the pickup and sat next to him. He had seen her on the school bus, but had never talked to her. "Sandy is going to help us spread hay in the hay loft tomorrow while you rest your ankle," said Mrs. Knudsen. Not knowing what to say to Sandy, Johnny blurted out, "Would you like to go fishing in the creek behind the Knudsens' farm sometime," asked Johnny? "Sure, I like to fish," said Sandy. Johnny said, "Tomorrow, when you finish your work in the hay loft, why don't you meet me on the bridge, behind the house?" "Okay, I'll be there," she said.

Mrs. Knudsen dropped Johnny off at his house and waved as she went down the red dirt road. Sandy also waived and smiled, which made Johnny feel good. Johnny hadn't thought too much about girls before, but she had gotten his attention. Sandy had stirred up some kind of feelings in Johnny which he couldn't explain. When Johnny went into the house, his mother asked him, "Why are you limping?" Johnny explained what had happened and told her how Mrs. Knudsen had taken care of him and that she had given him a ride home.

The next day, Johnny dug some worms from the moist, rich soil behind the barn. Putting the can of worms in his backpack along with the fish hooks, sinkers, line and a few cookies, Johnny walked to the bridge, over the creek. Once he was there, he cut fishing poles from the tall, slim elder bushes, growing along the banks of the creek. He cut two poles about five feet long and tied six feet of fishing line to the end of each pole. A small fishing hook, used for brook trout, and a sinker were attached to the other end of the line. The day was warm and the late afternoon sun felt good. Johnny leaned back against one of the bridge supports, pulled his hat over his eyes and fell asleep.

He was awakened by someone calling his name. It was Sandy who had finished her hay spreading chores in the Knudsen's barn. "Wake up," Johnny, she shouted, as she approached the bridge. "Howdy, I'm glad you came," said Johnny. "I made us a couple of fishing poles," he said. Let's see if we can catch some fish," said Sandy with a smile. Bringing the poles over to the center of the bridge, Johnny gave her one of them. Taking the can of worms from his backpack, Johnny put a worm on each hook. The water was running about three feet below the bridge. Sitting on the bridge with their feet hanging over the side, they dropped the lines into the water. "How did it go in the hay loft today," asked Johnny? "It was hot and dusty," said Sandy. "I got a bite!" shouted Sandy, as she pulled up a nice brook trout about a foot long. Johnny grabbed the trout and took it off the hook. It was a beautiful fish and Johnny was about to put it in a cloth sack, when Sandy said, "Let the fish go and let's go swimming." Johnny released the fish and asked Sandy, "Where do you want to go swimming?" "I'm hot and I thought the creek water would feel refreshing; the cold water should feel good on your ankle as well," said Sandy.

The water under the bridge was shallow and slow moving; it was ideal for swimming. Taking off her shoes, Sandy jumped off the bridge into the creek. She splashed around in the cold pool of water. "Come on in, the water feels great," said Sandy. "Removing his boots and keeping a sock over his bandage, Johnny slid into the water off the bridge. The water was very cold and jolted Johnny's system! He didn't want to let on to Sandy that the water was way too cold for him, because he didn't want her to think he was a sissy. As Sandy splashed around in the water, she asked, "Doesn't this feel good?" "It doesn't get much better than this," said Johnny, as he gazed at the beautiful blue sky full of white fluffy clouds. After a couple of minutes in the cold water, Johnny's wounds stopped throbbing. The cold water had made the swelling go down and the pressure was relieved on his ankle. "You're right, replied Johnny. "My ankle feels a lot better in this icy, cold water." After splashing each other, they decided to get out and dry off. The creek had formed a sand bar just below the pool of water. Climbing out of the creek and sitting on the sand bar felt great, as they basked in the rays of the warm afternoon sun. "You look like a drowned rat," teased Johnny. "Well, you look like a wounded drowned rat", joshed Sandy. "It felt so good to jump into the cold water after sweating and being covered with dust from the hay," remarked Sandy; now, I feel clean. Sandy did look clean and fresh after the swim, thought Johnny. She was a very pretty girl and in great shape, due to the hard work she had to do on her parents' farm. Sitting next to each other, on the sand bar, Sandy turned toward Johnny, picked up his hand and held it in her hands. She said, "I see you on the school bus every day during the school year, but we have never talked." I have noticed you on the bus as well, but didn't know what to say to you," said Johnny. "We're talking now, so what do you think of me," asked Sandy? "I think you are nice to talk to and you're pretty," said Johnny. "That's what I wanted to hear," said Sandy. "Even for a drowned, injured rat, I think you are very handsome," said Sandy. "Will you be coming back tomorrow," asked Johnny? "No," said Sandy, I'll be working on my farm, helping my parents with hay making." "I have an old car; maybe I could drive over to see you sometime," said Johnny. "Come by tomorrow evening after seven o'clock," said Sandy. ""I'll be there," said Johnny. Sandy jumped up and said, "I have to be headed home now and I hope your ankle gets better real soon." She gave him a flirtatious glance as she looked back over her shoulder. She waved goodbye to Johnny, crossed the bridge and disappeared over the hill. Johnny felt something new inside him when he was with Sandy. He was looking forward to seeing her again tomorrow evening.

Getting up from the sandbar, Johnny went to the bridge, where he gathered the fishing poles he had made and stored them at the end of the bridge. He sat down in the middle of the bridge dangling his feet over the side. Reaching into his backpack, he took out the cookies he had brought along. He had intended to share the cookies his mother had made with Sandy, but their swim had interrupted the fishing and he forgot to mention them to her. It was very pleasant just sitting there listening to the water, rushing over the rocks, below the bridge. He was thinking about Sandy and how happy things had turned out with her. He couldn't wait until tomorrow evening to see her.

Flinging his backpack on his back, Johnny started for home. While walking up the big hill from the river, Johnny was startled by a mother black bear and her two cubs. They crossed the road about one hundred yards ahead. The mother bear just glanced at Johnny then followed her cubs across the road and into the forest. He was very relieved that she just lumbered along with her cubs and had not come after him.

Reaching home, Johnny sat in the yard with his back against an apple tree. The apples would start to ripen in a couple of weeks; just thinking about their sweet, crisp taste made his mouth water. A hawk was circling overhead and seemed to be floating in mid-air. It must be nice to be able to fly, thought Johnny. Gazing into the setting sun, Johnny dozed off but was awakened by his dog. Butch had come over and laid his head in Johnny's lap. Johnny liked to throw a stick for Butch to go fetch; however, Butch was not a retriever and would just look at Johnny in puzzlement, wondering why his master would throw away something he already had.

Johnny went in the house and was greeted by the aroma of beef pot roast, potatoes, carrots and onions, simmering on the wood stove. His mother said, "We'll eat as soon as your father gets home." Fresh, homemade bread was setting in the warmer oven, along with wild raspberry pie. These succulent aromas made Johnny hungry. The garden vegetables were fresh and ready to go with the meal.

After enjoying the hearty evening meal, Johnny sat outside on the front porch, to listen to the sounds of the forest. He enjoyed the cool, fresh-smelling breeze on his face. He could hear the barking and yipping of coyotes in the distance. Then he heard a strange, far off sound; the coyotes went silent. Johnny had heard this sound before; it was like a combination of a wolf's howl and a mountain lion's scream. Whatever it was out there made the unnerving sound four more times. Everything became silent each time after the screams occurred. It made goose bumps rise on Johnny's arms. Even the fur on Butch's neck bristled, as his keen hearing picked up the mysterious sounds as well. Soon the typical sounds of a summer evening returned. With a full stomach and thoughts of Sandy on his mind, Johnny fell into a deep sleep, while sitting in the lawn chair, on his front porch.

The next morning when Johnny woke up, the sun was just about to break in the horizon. His ankle still hurt, but it was getting better. He hobbled around, feeding the chickens and gathering the eggs. He also filled the wood box, on the front porch with dry wood. He cleaned his old car so it would look good when he went to see Sandy. Johnny had already gotten permission from his parents to drive over to Sandy's that evening.

Johnny picked a beautiful red rose out of his mother's flower garden, to give to Sandy. He picked a long, purple Iris to bring to her mother. When Johnny pulled into Sandy's driveway, she came out of the front door of her house to greet him. Her long hair fell onto her shoulders and looked beautiful. She was wearing a red pantsuit and looked very pretty. Johnny said, "Here's a rose to match your pantsuit." Sandy took the rose, smelled the aroma of the petals and said, "I need to put this in a vase of water." Come on in and say hello to my parents," said Sandy. When he met her mother, he gave her the purple Iris; she was pleased that he was this thoughtful. She asked Johnny about his ankle. "My ankle still hurts a little, but it should be fine in a couple of days. Sandy's father, Duncan, said, "I know your parents from having met them at town meetings. I know your two older brothers who helped me to harvest oats, over the past years. And now, it's a real pleasure meeting you."

Sandy's mother said, "Johnny would you like a piece of strawberry pie with some fresh homemade ice cream?" "Yes, please, that sounds good," replied Johnny. Sandy said, "Johnny, why don't we eat our pie and ice cream at the table outside, in the apple orchard?" "Okay, said Johnny, if it's alright with your parents." "Sure," said Sandy's father, "It's nice and cool outside." Sitting at the table under the apple trees, Sandy said, "I'm so glad you came over." "I was looking forward to it. And I'm glad I got to meet your parents," said Johnny.

"There's a group of young people, from my church, gathering at Blue Lake this Sunday afternoon. We are going to swim, cook hot dogs, and roast marshmallows over an open fire. Would you like to go," asked Johnny? "Yes, let me ask my parents", said Sandy. She ran into her house for a moment and came out with a big smile. "They said yes, but I have to be home before dark," said Sandy. Johnny carried the dishes into the house and thanked Sandy's mother for the pie and ice cream. "Thanks for letting Sandy go with me to the lake on Sunday; I promise to take very good care of her," said Johnny. "You're welcome. We'll see you on Sunday," said Mrs. Sawyer. Johnny drove home feeling happy about his evening with the Sawyers. He was already growing very fond of Sandy and he was thankful that her parents both seemed to like and accept him as well.

It was a sunny, warm day on Sunday when Johnny picked Sandy up to go to the lake. Sandy was ready and came out of the house carrying a basket and had a quilt under one arm. "I thought we could sit on this old picnic quilt after our swim," said Sandy. "Good idea," said Johnny, who had brought one large towel. "I brought the hot dogs and marshmallows," said Johnny. "And I brought some potato salad, banana pudding, and peanut butter cookies to share," said Sandy. Johnny thought she was wonderful to have done all that.

Pulling up at the lake, Johnny could see some of his friends already down at the beach. "There are restrooms by the water where we can change into our swimming suits," said Johnny. "Okay, and I'll bring the quilt and suntan lotion," said Sandy. Johnny and Sandy walked down to the beach, greeting everyone they knew. "Let's get changed and go for a swim," said Johnny.

When Sandy came out of the restroom in her swimsuit, Johnny couldn't believe how great she looked. He couldn't take his eyes off Sandy and was trying hard not to stare. Just then, Johnny heard a familiar voice calling his name. It was Sam with a cute, dark-haired girl by his side. "Johnny and Sandy, I'd like you to meet Gloria," said Sam. "Very nice to meet you," said Johnny and Sandy. I met Gloria at the feed store," said Sam. "Her uncle owns the store and Gloria is working for him during the summer." "Gloria is from Chicago and enjoys being out in the country during the summer," said Sam. "Let's all go down to the water for a swim," said Johnny. The water was clear and cold, as the lake was spring-fed; everyone shivered a little when first entering the water. After a couple of minutes, the water felt great. There was a floating raft put in the swimming area by the township. "Let's swim out to the raft," said Sam. Everyone agreed and they all swam out to it. After a few dives off the raft into the deep, clear water, everyone climbed back onto the raft for a rest. Those already lounging on the raft noticed a group of girls, near the shore, starting to swim in their direction. About halfway to the raft, one of the girls yelled, "I can't make it," then she disappeared under the water. Johnny and Sam had taken water safety training the previous summer. The boys were good, strong swimmers and had learned how to rescue a drowning person.

"Let's go get her, Sam," yelled Johnny. The boys dove off the raft, in the direction of the drowning girl. The girl broke through the top of the water in front of the boys, then disappeared again." "I have her spotted," said Sam. Sam dove underwater and came up with the girl. Johnny grabbed the girl when she surfaced with Sam. Johnny said, "She's not breathing. Let's get her to shore." Johnny and Sam pulled the lifeless girl to shore and placed her down on the sand. "Sam, you compress her chest and I'll give her mouth-to-mouth resuscitation," said Johnny. The boys worked fast, but the girl wasn't responding. Johnny remembered his dad had once picked him up upside down and squeezed him to get the water out of his lungs. "Sam, pick her up upside down and squeeze her," said Johnny. Sam was strong and had no problem picking up the girl and giving her a hard squeeze. Johnny continued mouth-to-mouth resuscitation; soon the girl coughed up water and drew a series of deep breaths. "Sam, lay her back down on the sand. Let's roll her over on her stomach so she can cough up the rest of the water that's in her lungs," said Johnny. After several minutes of hard coughing, the girl got up on her hands and knees and began to breathe okay. By this time, everyone had swum back to shore and had gathered around her to ask if she was alright. The girl said that she felt fine and thanked the boys for saving her life.

As it turned out, the girls were part of a musical group from Minnesota, who were

touring the Upper Peninsula of Michigan. They would be performing at a local town hall and invited everyone to their performance that evening. "I'm sure it would be fun, but we have to get back home before dark and can't spend the night out," said Johnny. "Thanks again for your help today," said one of the girls. "You're welcome," said Johnny. Sam said, "Be careful and enjoy the rest of your trip."

"What you and Sam did was amazing," said Sandy. Thank goodness we took water safety training last summer," said Sam. "Sandy, let's sit down on your quilt and dry off," said Johnny. "Gloria and I are going up the hill to take a break," said Sam. "See you at the fire pit later," said Johnny.

The sun felt good after coming out of the cold water, thought Johnny, while sitting on Sandy's soft cotton patchwork quilt. Sandy said, "We had better put on some suntan lotion to keep from getting sunburned. Would you rub some lotion on my back?" "Sure," said Johnny. After lying in the sun for a while, Johnny said, "I'm getting hungry." "Let's go and see if someone has started the fire," said Sandy.

When Sandy and Johnny got back to the picnic area, they were glad that someone had already started a fire and others had already begun roasting wieners and toasting marshmallows. Sandy went to the car and got her picnic basket, while Johnny whittled sticks for roasting the hot dogs and marshmallows. Sam and Gloria came down from the big hill to the fire with Sam carrying a cooler with bottles of homemade root beer. Somebody had brought a radio and it was tuned to a local radio station that was playing Golden Oldies. After eating, some of the group began to dance. Sandy said, "Johnny, would you like to dance?" "I don't know how," said Johnny. "Come on, I'll teach you," said Sandy. "Okay, I'll try," said Johnny. Sandy said, "I'll show you the steps and then you can try to move to the music." "Remember, I still have a sore ankle, so we will have to slow dance," said Johnny. "Hold my right hand with your left hand and put your right arm around my waist," said Sandy. "I'll lead and you just follow my footsteps," said Sandy. Moving to the music, Johnny was able to follow Sandy after just a few tries. "This is easier than I thought," said Johnny. "Now follow me without looking at your feet," said Sandy. After stepping on Sandy's feet a few times, Johnny was able to follow her without looking at his feet. "You're doing just fine," said Sandy. "Thanks for the lesson," said Johnny, as he looked at Sandy with his twinkling sky-blue eyes.

After dancing, everyone ate again. They told Sandy they loved her potato salad, banana pudding, and peanut butter cookies. Sandy just smiled and blushed. She was happy to have been brought into this nice group of young people. Johnny said, "We'd better be going, Sandy, as it will be getting dark in a couple of hours." The gathering had been fun with singing, joke telling, and dancing. Sam put out the fire, as others started gathering up their stuff and loading their cars to go home. Sandy and Gloria said they had enjoyed themselves and perhaps they could all do this again soon. Of course, Sam and Johnny agreed.

Johnny and Sandy arrived at Sandy's farm before dark which pleased her parents. Sandy's father was outside working on a tractor and asked if they had a good time. Sandy said, "Yes," and told him how Johnny and Sam had saved a drowning girl. "That's great," said Sandy's father. "How did you know what to do," he asked? Sam and I took a water safety training class last summer," replied Johnny. "I've got to be getting home," said Johnny. "I still have some chores to do," he said. "I had a good time," said Sandy. "So did I," said Johnny. He wanted to give Sandy a big hug, but with her father standing right there, he decided against it. Johnny had developed strong feelings for Sandy and he thought Sandy felt the same way toward him. Johnny waved goodbye, as he pulled out of the driveway. Sandy and her father waved back until Johnny was out of sight. All the way home, Johnny kept thinking about Sandy and he knew he wanted to be with her as much as possible. Once he got home, Johnny had to hurry to feed the chickens and fill the wood box before dark.

The next morning, Johnny went to work, in the woods peeling the bark off hemlock trees; his father had a contract to fill two railroad cars with peeled hemlock logs. Johnny's ankle still hurt a little, but not enough to stay home from working in the woods. Johnny kept thinking about Sandy which kept his mind off his sore ankle. Johnny would be busy working all week and wouldn't get to see Sandy until the following Sunday.

Sunday came and Johnny drove over to Sandy's farm to see her. When Johnny arrived at Sandy's place, he saw her sitting at a table under the apple trees. She didn't get up when Johnny approached her, which was out-of-character and unusual behavior for her. "How are you doing, Sandy," asked Johnny? Sandy looked up and had tears in her eyes. "What's wrong," asked Johnny? Sandy stood up and said, "Let's go for a walk." She took Johnny's hand and led him down the path, to the hay barn. Johnny asked Sandy again what was wrong and she looked at him with tears running down her cheeks. Sandy said, "Come in the barn where we can talk." She took both of Johnny's hands and squeezed them. "My father told me he just sold the farm and we will be moving to Minnesota next week," said Sandy. "He said his doctor told him that he has a bad heart and should give up farming. He accepted a job at a manufacturing plant in Minneapolis," said Sandy.

"I can't believe this is happening, just when I found someone who I like," said Sandy. She dropped Johnny's hands and wrapped her arms around him hugging him tight. Johnny was stunned and hugged her back, as she cried with her head on his shoulder. Tears welled up in Johnny's eyes at the devastating news. He said, "I like you, too, Sandy and this news makes me feel heartsick." Johnny released Sandy from his arms and wiped the tears off her cheeks. "This is terrible news, but we can still keep in touch by writing to each other." said Johnny. "Yes, I know. But it won't be the same when I can't see you," said Sandy. "I love you Johnny," said Sandy. "I love you too, said Johnny. "I have to get back to the house and help with the packing," said Sandy. "Okay," said Johnny. "When will you be leaving?" "Saturday morning," said Sandy. "Do you need help with packing or anything," asked Johnny? "No, everything has been arranged," said Sandy. "I'm going to do something that I've wanted to do ever since I met you," said Johnny. He pulled Sandy close to him and gave her a tender kiss on her lips. Releasing her, Johnny said, "I'm glad I did it." "I'm glad you kissed me too," said Sandy. I will always cherish this moment," said Sandy. "I'll come over Saturday morning before you leave, to say good-bye," said Johnny. "I'll be waiting for you," said Sandy.

Johnny and Sandy walked back to his car holding hands. He got in his car and waved good-bye, as he was backing out, down the long driveway. With tears streaming down her face, Sandy waved back and blew him a kiss. Johnny drove home with tears in his eyes and an empty feeling in the pit of his stomach; he was thinking of how much he was going to miss Sandy. She was the first girl he had ever kissed and that was so very significant to him. He cared for her in a way he had never cared for anyone else. He felt so committed to her; he wanted to take care of her and protect her. He couldn't stand the thought of them being separated by so many miles. All he knew was that he wanted her in his life and in his future.

When Saturday came, Johnny got up before daylight and told his parents that he was going to say good-bye to Sandy. Arriving at Sandy's farm, Johnny saw that the trailer was packed and they were ready to go. Johnny said good-bye to Sandy's parents who were already in the station wagon. Sandy was outside waiting for him. Their eyes locked on each other for a moment that seemed like an eternity. Feeling sad, Johnny gave Sandy a tight hug and a quick peck of a kiss. Sandy got into the car, rolled down the window, and said, "I'll write to you as soon as I get there. I'll miss you, Johnny." Johnny stood in the road and waved to Sandy until she was out-of-sight.

Feeling sad, Johnny got in his car and started to drive home. Passing Sam's farm, he decided to stop and see him to tell him how sad he was. Sam was just coming out of the barn when Johnny pulled into the driveway. Johnny stopped the car and told him that Sandy had just left a short while ago. "I know you like her and she likes you too," said Sam. "It was tough seeing her go, but she promised to write," said Johnny. "Sandy has an aunt and uncle in a neighboring town and said she could visit them, so we could see each other from time-to-time," said Johnny.

"So when will Gloria be going back to Chicago," asked Johnny? "She will be going back next month just before school starts," answered Sam. "Will she be coming back anytime soon to visit her uncle," asked Johnny? "Yes, she will be coming back here over the Christmas Holidays and for New Year's Eve," said Sam. "That's nice; I don't know if Sandy will come up to see her aunt and uncle at that time," said Johnny. "It has been a great summer for us, Johnny. We got to meet and go out with some nice girls," said Sam. "You're right, Sam. Even though I miss Sandy already, I had a great time with her," said Johnny. "Think on the positive side and tell yourself that she will come back to visit," said Sam. "Sam, I think we need to go on another adventure to get me out of my sad state of mind," said Johnny. "Good idea," said Sam. Let's decide what we want to do next week," said Sam. Johnny told Sam good-bye and then drove home thinking about Sandy and when they would see each other again.

CHAPTER 8
BULL MOOSE STALKING

Johnny and his buddy, Sam, decided they could make some extra money trapping beaver. By the time beaver trapping season opened, they had acquired all the equipment they needed. Provisions such as food and emergency supplies were ready for the backpacks to be carried on their adventure. Summer sausage, homemade bread, canned sardines, coffee grounds and peppermints made up the food choices. Gauze, tape and iodine were the medical supplies in case of cuts or scratches. With all the combined supplies and equipment, the backpacks weighed about forty pounds each.

The beaver trapping season lasted two weeks during the month of March. There was still about two feet of snow covering the ground so snowshoes had to be used to walk to the beaver dams and rivers. Excited about the coming adventure, Johnny said to Sam, "I think we're going to get our limit of beaver pelts and get a good price for them." Sam replied, "I think you're right and I can't wait to start setting out traps." Johnny's old Ford car was ready to go with big snow and mud tires on the rear. A set of tire chains, along with a jack and spare tire were in the trunk. The snowshoes, axe and a shovel were also loaded into the trunk of the car for added safety. Trapping licenses had been purchased and the anticipation of the adventure was exciting.

After a restless night's sleep, Johnny got up at four o'clock a.m., raring to go. There were coals still glowing in the kitchen cook stove, so Johnny added some wood and got the fire going. The kitchen warmed up fast and Johnny's mother appeared in the doorway. You must be excited about your trapping adventure," she said. Johnny's mother made a hardy breakfast. She fixed ham, eggs, toast from homemade bread, orange juice, boysenberry jam, and hot tea. Johnny thought to himself how lucky he was to have a wonderful mother like this. She was able to function so well in their old, outdated kitchen with the wood stove. Someday, he wanted to give her an entire new kitchen with all new appliances. His mother asked, "Do you have matches?" Is your sleeping bag and a shotgun in your car?" "No, I forgot," said Johnny. "I was too excited about my first day of beaver trapping." "Well, it's a good thing I reminded you. It's cold at night and you need something warm in case of an emergency," she said. "We don't plan on being outside after dark and should be home by six o'clock this evening," said Johnny. He added the sleeping bag and shotgun in the trunk of his car. He put matches into his backpack as well.

After breakfast, Johnny said goodbye to his mother and went out to start his old car. It was so cold the snow crunched beneath his insulated boots. He scraped the ice off the windshield and got in his car. The thermometer said it was ten degrees below zero. On the fifth try, it started. He sat in the driveway and let the car idle for about ten minutes to heat up the engine, as well as the interior. Once his heater started warming, it soon became very toasty inside. The morning was beautiful with the moonlight shining on the snow. The morning was quiet except for the occasional cracking pop of a frozen maple tree. When the sap in the maple trees froze, it caused them to split and it would sound like a rifle shot. The dirt roads were bare, but frozen and driving on them made a dull roar beneath the tires.

Sam lived about a mile away. He was all packed and ready to go when Johnny arrived. It was now about six o'clock a.m.;

Sam had already finished milking the cows and had done his morning chores. The sun would be coming up in about an hour and a half and it would take the sting out of the bitter cold, crisp air. "Hello," hollered Sam, as Johnny's car pulled into the yard. "Are you ready to go trap some beaver," asked Johnny? "You betcha," said Sam. Let's get this jalopy on the road!" Sam brought a big thermos full of hot cocoa and some warm, homemade pastry; he poured a steaming cup of cocoa for each of them and off they went. They both enjoyed the cocoa and pastries, as they drove along, on this brisk, cold morning. After driving a short distance from Sam's house, the boys came upon several deer just standing in the road. They were taking advantage of walking down the dirt road instead of tramping through the snow. Johnny slowed the car down and waited for the deer to move to the side of the road so he could pass them.

The area where the beaver trapping would be done was about thirty-five miles into the forest. There were no farms or houses along these roads, as it was state and national forest land. A few old abandoned homesteads and an occasional hunting camp were scattered along these forest highways. The roads were covered with snow and nobody had driven on them since the deer hunting season, at the end of November. The Forest Service plowed these roads through the deer hunting season and would wait until April to start grading them again. Since no one lived out in these remote areas, in the winter, there was no reason to keep these roads open. Johnny's sturdy old car, with the big snow tires, had no problem going through the occasional snowdrift. It was kind of fun to see a snowdrift two or three feet high and to burst right through it! Spring had caused some brief periods of thawing weather, so the creeks, rivers, and beaver dams had some flowing water running through them.

Driving as far back into the forest as possible, Johnny said, "I guess this is as good a place as any to stop." "Let's get our stuff out and get those traps set," said Sam. The snow in the woods was about two and one half feet deep, so snowshoes would be needed to get to the dams that were in the valleys. "We have a little crust on the snow, so it should be easy snowshoeing," said Johnny. Having fished this area for trout in the summer, the area was familiar. It would be about one half mile downhill to the dams. With the heavy packs on their backs, the crunchy snow held up pretty well under the snowshoes. The air was crisp, but after a few minutes of walking, it was comfortable out in the cold.

The first dam they arrived at was covered with ice and snow; there was just a trickle of water running over it. In the deep, narrow valley, the sun didn't have much opportunity to shine on the dams to thaw the ice and to let the water flow. There was no sign of beaver coming out of their houses; the ice was still too thick. "We can't set traps in conditions like this," remarked Sam. The sun was just peaking over the top of the valley and the warmth of the rays felt so good. "I think we should make some coffee and decide where we should go to find some open water," said Johnny. "Good idea," said Sam. "We will have to find a shallower valley that has had more sun during the day," said Sam. "You get the water and I'll make a fire," said Johnny. Gathering dry branches off a nearby spruce tree, Johnny started a small fire. The heat from the flames felt good. The snow beneath the crust was loose and easy to kick out of the way down to the frozen ground. Sam brought a small coffee pot full of water and put some coffee grounds in it. While waiting for the fire to die down, the boys discussed where they should go next to look for open water. "Maybe the area around Spruce River would be good," said Johnny. "Loggers were in there last year clearing trees; maybe the sun has melted some of the ice." "That sounds like a good choice," said Sam. "That river runs east and west so it gets sun all day long," remarked Sam. The fire had died down and there were some nice red coals on which to set the coffee pot. In a few minutes, the water began to boil and the smell of coffee in the crisp cold air was great. Johnny got some bread and summer sausage out of his pack and made a couple of sandwiches. The sandwiches and hot coffee were a perfect blend in the outdoors.

The morning sun was now shinning down in full force and its warmth felt good. Leaning back on their packs, Sam and Johnny closed their eyes and enjoyed a rest by the warm fire. They were startled by a pack of coyotes yipping while in pursuit of a rabbit. The rabbit darted into a hollow log and the coyotes gave up the chase. The coyotes were surprised to look across the beaver dam and see two people by a fire. After studying the situation for less than a minute, the coyotes disappeared into the dense evergreens.

After putting out the fire, Sam said, "I'll race you to the top of the hill. "Okay, you're on," said Johnny, as he was putting on his snowshoes. It was a half mile to the top of the hill and with forty pound packs on their backs, walking would be tough. They both started off on a slow jog, staying about even. A third of the way up the hill, both were now sweating and had opened their jackets and a couple of buttons on their shirts. With their legs tired from the heavy packs, the slow jog had now turned to a walk. Johnny stopped for a rest to catch his breath and Sam now took the lead.

"I've got you now," hollered Sam, as he kept trudging up the hill. Johnny was trying hard to catch up when he heard Sam yell, "Yikes," and saw him tumbling backwards in the snow. Sam was on his back with his snowshoes up in the air. One of his snowshoes had caught on a branch underneath the snow and had tripped him. "Are you okay," yelled Johnny? "I just got a snow bath from all the snow that got inside my jacket and shirt," replied Sam. Swinging his snowshoes toward the bottom of the hill, Sam was able to get back up on his feet. Shaking the snow from his clothes, inside and out, he hollered, "Okay, I'm ready to go again." Sam's fall gave Johnny the lead. With cramping leg muscles and sweat-soaked shirts, the boys reached the top of the hill at about the same time. "I won," hollered Johnny and Sam responded with, "No, I won." It was hard to tell who was on the top of the hill first, so they decided that they both had won. After laughing about such an exhausting race, they both collapsed in the snow.

Soon, the sweaty clothes started to feel cold. It had not been a good idea to get sweaty in this cold weather. A person could get hypothermia with no dry clothes under these conditions. They decided they had better go back to the car to dry their clothes. Removing the packs and the snowshoes, they stowed them away in the car. The heater in the car would sure give them enough heat to get warm. Once in the car, Johnny turned the key and pressed the starter button, but the car wouldn't start; the battery had become low due to the extreme cold. "Oh no," said Sam. "What do you think we should do now?" "We had better gather wood and build a big fire," said Johnny. "Looks like we're going to spend the night out here," said Sam. "We will have to dry our long underwear to keep from freezing tonight," said Johnny.

They gathered plenty of wood and built a big fire; one that would burn the better part of the night. Evergreens were cut down to build a circle around the fire. Evergreen boughs were spread out on the ground and the sleeping bags were rolled out on top of them. Extra wood for the fire was gathered and placed inside the circle of evergreens. The snowshoes were stuck upright near the fire to hang the damp clothes on to dry. The air was still and the sky was a beautiful, deep shade of blue. It would take almost an hour to dry the clothes so the boys undressed and hung the clothes on the snowshoes to dry. The sun would be going down soon and the temperature would plummet well below zero degrees. Getting in the cold sleeping bags was not easy, but once inside it didn't take long to get warm.

After about an hour, the wet clothes were smoky, but dry. The boys got into the dry clothes and it sure felt good. They ate canned sardines, homemade bread, and summer sausage, along with more coffee made from melted snow for their supper. As dusk was approaching, howling wolves could be heard in the distance. The shotguns were taken out of the car and placed by the sleeping bags. The howl of a wolf is exciting to hear, but still a little scary. They looked at each other because they both knew they had to be aware and cautious.

The sun, having disappeared, brought quite a chill to the air. No wind was blowing and the sun had been replaced by a full moon. The sky being clear, made the stars stand out like diamonds in the sky. Once in a while, a shooting star would streak across the sky, followed by a brilliant white trail. The wolves were getting closer, as their howls were growing louder. They had zoned in on the boys' location. More wood was added to the fire for warmth and protection from the wolves. The loud popping of the frozen trees rang through the still, cold air. The temperature had dropped to twenty degrees below zero, according to a thermometer which was kept in the car. Sam said, "Johnny, my sleeping bag is cold on the side away from the fire and I'm starting to shiver." Sam's sleeping bag wasn't designed for below zero weather, but Johnny's was rated for minus forty degrees. Johnny's bag was a cocoon style, Navy surplus bag and had room for one person. Johnny said, "Sam, there's enough room for half of your body in my bag, so put your cold side in my bag and keep your warm side toward the fire." The warmth of Johnny's sleeping bag kept Sam warm on one side, while the fire kept Sam's other side warm. Wood was added to the fire every hour or so until morning. It had been a fretful night, but a safe one.

The roar of a train broke the morning silence. The tracks were about two miles away. Johnny said, "Let's make coffee and then head for the railroad tracks." With the train going through, the tracks would be clear of snow and it would make walking easier. The food was gone except for some peppermints. After the boys had their coffee, they headed for the tracks. They decided to leave the snowshoes in the car and take the shotguns. The snow was about a foot deep beneath the cover of the pine forest. It would be a long, thirty mile walk home along the tracks. Arriving at the tracks, it was good to see the bare rail and crossties. Walking down a railroad track is not easy unless one has very long legs. The crossties are spaced a little further apart than the average man's stride, so one has to take longer strides to land on the ties. Sam had the sense to grab the coffee pot and coffee before they left the car.

No one knew where they had gone, so their parents didn't know where to look for them. When the boys didn't return the night before, a search party was underway the next morning. The railroad tracks crossed streams so about noon the boys went down to one of the creeks, broke through the ice and got some water for coffee. They built a small fire between the ties and the rails of the track. They figured they had walked about eight or nine miles by noon and would have to spend another night out in the cold without the sleeping bags. After having the hot coffee, they decided to walk for three more hours which would get them about halfway home.

Sam said, "It's going to be another sub-zero night and we will be cold even with a fire." "Why don't we build two fires and lie down between them," remarked Johnny. "Good idea," said Sam. "We can lie on evergreen boughs to give us insulation. Let's make the fires on the railroad bed and without any wind, the flames should go straight up," suggested Johnny. Boughs from evergreens were laid down for a bed and two fires with extra wood were started. It was another cold night, but with the two fires going, sleep was possible. The fires died down often and new wood had to be added throughout the night. The rest of the peppermints tasted good, since they were the last edible items the boys had left.

At daybreak, the boys started walking around a bend. A moose was coming in their direction, down the center of the tracks. When the boys saw it, they knew to get out of the moose's way. "We have to get up in a tree," said Johnny. Since the shotguns were almost useless against a moose, the boys got off the track and climbed up about twenty feet, in a birch tree. It was a big bull moose who had lost his rack during the winter. He was being pursued by a pack of wolves. The wolves couldn't catch him because he could run faster. The moose passed the tree where the boys were hiding, with the pack of wolves a couple hundred yards behind. When the wolves got to the tree where the boys were, they stopped. The pack of hungry wolves surrounded the tree the boys were in.

The wolves looked up at the boys snarling and showing their fangs. The wolves knew they couldn't climb the tree to get the boys, so they lay underneath the tree. The wolves were going to wait out the boys and attack them when they came down. "Sam, we have to chase those wolves away; otherwise, we will freeze up here in the tree," said Johnny. "Let's fire a shot over them to see if they scatter," said Sam. "They don't look rabid…just hungry," said Johnny. Sam fired a shot over the wolves and they jumped up to their feet snarling. The leader of the pack began leaping up at the base of the tree showing his teeth. "It looks as if they're not going to leave," said Johnny. "If we shoot the pack leader, the rest may run away," said Sam. "I hate to do it, but I think it's the chance for survival we have to take," said Johnny. Johnny took aim on the leader of the pack and fired, killing the big wolf. The rest of the pack fled after seeing their leader killed. The pack headed for the railroad track and continued in the direction the moose had taken. The boys climbed down from the tree and went back to the tracks.

Johnny said, "We should be able to walk out of here by this evening." The sky was black and starless. Wind was starting to whistle through the trees. "It looks like a snow storm is coming our way. We had better find some kind of shelter soon," said Sam. "There's a deer hunting camp a few miles further down these tracks," said Johnny. The cold wind was increasing from the north and it began snowing harder and harder. The snow pelted the boys, stinging their faces. Snow began piling up on the railroad tracks and it became easier to walk backward rather than forward. "Do you think we should go into the pines and wait until this storm passes," asked Sam? "No," replied Johnny. "I think we should continue until we get to the hunting shack. The snow will continue to get deeper and pretty soon, we won't be able to walk at all. We won't be able to spend the night out in the open in this kind of weather. We have to get to shelter pretty soon."

With the snow coming down in heavy sheets and the wind swirling, it was becoming hard to walk; bending forward and looking straight down at the tracks was how they could keep moving forward. "I'm getting tired and just want to sit down in the snow and rest," said Sam. "No, we have to keep moving, or we will freeze to death out here," said Johnny. Just then, Johnny looked up and there was the hunting camp he remembered. "Sam, we're here," exclaimed Johnny! "We made it," yelled Sam. Walking up to the camp, Johnny noticed a padlock on the front door. There was no back door, but there were windows on each side. Sam tried one of the windows, but it was nailed shut. Johnny tried the other window and it opened. The boys crawled into the camp through the window. A kerosene lantern was on the table which Sam lit; the light was nice to have. There was a wood stove with wood and kindling nearby, in a wood box. Johnny built a fire in it and the heat felt so good, after coming out of the winter storm. The canisters in the cupboard had flour, sugar and coffee grounds in them. No canned food, as it would have frozen. When they opened a bread box, they found two dry fruit-filled buns in it. Sam heated the buns on the stove and bit into one. "Tastes good; a little dry, but edible," he said. Johnny ate one and thought it was delicious because he was so hungry. They made coffee on the wood stove and enjoyed sipping it inside the warm cabin. The storm howled outside all night while the boys slept on the bare mattresses.

When daylight came, the sun was out and it was a beautiful day. "This will be a wonderful day to finish walking home," said Sam. A dreadful feeling came over Johnny, as he looked out the window. It was true that the sun looked beautiful in the sky with the fresh snow; however, the storm had dropped over two feet of new snow and the snowshoes were back in the car. And to make matters worse, the train tracks were covered with two feet of snow and with five foot snow drifts in some places. They were about six miles from home. In normal conditions, it would have taken four hours to walk; however, with no food and no way to walk through the high snow, survival became an issue. What if the train discontinued its runs on this track until the snow melted? And if more snow fell, it could be a month before these tracks would be used. "We have to walk out now. Let's look for something to use to walk on top of the snow," said Johnny. "What about the wooden bed slats that hold the mattress up on the bed," asked Sam? "They may work as skis," replied Johnny. The boys rounded the slats on one with a hunting knife. A can on a shelf provided nails to be driven into the sides of the slats. The nails would hold the leather shoe laces on their winter boots. With the boots secured to the makeshift bed slat skis, a way out was possible. The wind had hard-packed the snow and the homemade skis worked well. It was slow going when they left the camp, but the boys were now filled with enthusiasm. They left a note to whoever owned the camp saying that they would replace the bed slats before the next hunting season.

The sun was bright and the snow glistened pure white. There was no wind, so sliding over the snow seemed pleasant. It took about four hours to reach a plowed road and it sure felt good to get off those homemade skis. The boys could see the smoke coming from the chimney of a country bar where they could get some food. The people in the bar were very surprised to see the boys, as a search party had been organized to look for them. They were amazed as Johnny and Sam related the events of their journey. To spice it up a little, Sam said, "There were at least a dozen wolves in the pack that chased us." Johnny decided to add a little more spice to the story and said, "A bull moose chased us up a tree but was chased off by the pack of wolves."

After having a good breakfast of sausage, eggs, toast, juice and hot coffee, the boys were ready to go home. The snow plow driver had stopped at the bar for coffee and was headed toward the boys' homes, so he offered them a ride. "What about your car," asked the snow plow driver? It will have to stay there until the snow melts off the roads," said Johnny.

When the boys reached Sam's farm, there were a lot of cars parked everywhere. Their families, relatives, and friends had gathered there to form more search parties for the day. The neighbors and townspeople had heard about the missing boys and had all brought food over to the house. The table in the kitchen, dining room table, buffet, and all counter tops were laden with food from the concerned community. Everyone was thinking the worst and had just about resolved themselves to the grim fact that the boys could be dead by now. They thought perhaps the boys had either fallen in a beaver dam and couldn't get out, or could have died from hypothermia. Although nobody spoke of it, but were thinking they could have been eaten by hungry wolves. Johnny's mother had told everyone that Johnny was so positive that he and Sam would be back home by 6:00 p.m. on the first day, that he had taken enough food for one day. When the boys walked into Sam's kitchen, it was like they had risen from the dead. For a moment in time, there was absolute silence. Everyone was so relieved the boys had survived for three days and two nights in the sub-zero weather, there was not a dry eye among the group.

It was back to school the next day and having missed the first day of the week; an excuse from their parents was needed. Johnny's excuse read, "Please excuse Johnny's absence from school on Monday, as he was trapping beaver," signed by his mother.

The next week was springtime break in full force. The rivers were roaring and the ditches were full of rushing water. The road to Johnny's car was clear of snow, but water was washing across the roads in many places. Using Sam's father's tractor, the boys decided it was time to go get the car. It was slow and slushy going there, but with the big tires on the tractor, the water and mud were no problem. Reaching the car, the boys used jumper cables on the battery and the car started. Following the tractor down the muddy, wet road, Johnny was leery of the places where water was running across the road. The big tires of the tractor wouldn't notice if a washout had occurred across the road.

Sure enough, Johnny hit a washout at about fifteen miles per hour. The car came to a sudden stop as a wheel dropped into the washout. The jarring bent the metal axle between the wheels. Sam, noticing that Johnny had stopped and was blowing the car horn, figured something was wrong. Turning the tractor around, Sam went back and saw Johnny's car with the front end submerged in the water. "It looks like your tires weren't big enough to pass over the washout," said Sam. "I'll hook a chain to your front bumper, raise your car up with the hoist on the tractor and pull you out," Sam said. Once the car was out of the washout, the two front wheels were pointing in different directions. Unable to drive the car, Sam said, "Well, I guess I'll just have to raise your front wheels off the ground and tow you home." Johnny was thinking, as Sam towed his car toward home, about the beaver trapping experience. Not a trap was set and the car wouldn't start. Then, having to dry their long underwear after a race on snowshoes and having to spend two nights out in cold, sub-zero weather. Not to mention walking twenty-five miles down a railroad track and then fighting their way through a blizzard, going another six miles on homemade skis without any food and now topping it off by bending the front axle on his car. Was it worth all the effort to go beaver trapping, thought Johnny? Then he decided that even though the trapping wasn't worth it, the experience of the adventure was.

Upon arriving at Johnny's farm, the boys were met by Johnny's father who wondered why the car was being towed. Johnny explained what had happened and his father looked under the car. "The axle is bent but I can fix it," said his father. Johnny's father got a logging chain and a hydraulic truck jack and connected them to the axle. As he pumped the jack, the axle started to straighten. When he had finished, the axle was almost straight. Johnny thanked his father for fixing the axle. He also thanked Sam for towing his car for almost thirty miles. "Won't you come in for lunch, Sam," asked Johnny? "No thank you," said Sam. "I've got to get back home. "There's work to be done on the farm," Johnny's father said. "There's also plenty of work in the woods for you, young man," said his father. Cutting and hauling logs to the local mill was what Johnny's father meant. With beaver trapping season over, no traps had been set and no beaver had been caught. It had been another one of Johnny's great adventures.

CHAPTER 9
MOUNTAIN LION ATTACK

Not successful at trapping beaver Johnny decided that he would photograph them. He wanted to study the way they were able to build dams in moving water. There were many places to photograph beaver, but not many places to observe them in the actual building of a dam. He would have to find a location where food was available for the beavers. When food ran out in their present location, beavers would search for a new stream with more abundant food.

Another thought Johnny entertained, was to study how their houses were built. It was spring, the snow was gone, and the days were getting warm again. Bright sunshine would soon knock the dew off the grass, and the trees were beginning to bud. Green sprouts of grass were pushing through last year's layer of dead grass. Birds were flying around chirping, and squirrels were scurrying and chattering. The animals and birds in the forest were excited with the warm weather, after going through the long, harsh winter. Food was more accessible now and they were happy.

Johnny would have to find a place with new beaver chewings, indicating a move to a new area. He would have to travel deeper into the forest, beyond the usual dams. He knew of a remote area where a few hunters would go. It wasn't accessible by any motorized vehicle; walking was the way to get there. Even a person with good horsemanship would have a very difficult time maneuvering through the gullies and steep banks. Beavers on the other hand, would have no problem with this kind of environment.

There were stories of strange things happening in this particular remote area. Johnny figured they were tales passed on by hunters who wanted to keep people out of their prime turf. If a hunter were to shoot a deer, he would have to have it airlifted out by helicopter, due to the harsh terrain. The area Johnny was thinking about was five miles to the closest road. It would be a full day's trip just to walk in and back out. Johnny thought he would take his dog, Butch, along to warn him of any dangerous animals. Wolves, bears, and an occasional mountain lion were the main wild animals that Johnny could think of that he needed to be worried about. He would take a rifle with him in case he needed it for protection.

Johnny had filled his backpack with the necessary supplies and would go the next morning. School was not out for the summer, but tomorrow was Saturday. Work in the woods had not yet begun, so Johnny had a few free days to pursue his adventure. With his camera and two new rolls of film, Johnny was excited and ready to go. Butch loved going with Johnny on these outings and got excited when he saw Johnny filling his backpack.

The sun was not quite up, but Johnny was wide awake. Butch jumped up on Johnny's bed and licked his face; he was ready to go. "Are you ready for an adventure," Johnny asked Butch? Butch's tail started to wag in anticipation of their trip. Johnny's mother said, "I'll fix you and Butch a good breakfast before you leave." Johnny's mother cooked a good country breakfast of ham, eggs, buttered toast and oatmeal. Johnny got dressed. He put his gun and backpack by the door. He and Butch ate while Johnny visited with his mother at the breakfast table. "Where are you going," asked his mother? "To the northeast in that remote area that a few hunters frequent," said Johnny. "You be careful out there. You know the stories that people tell about that place," said Johnny's mother. "I think the hunters make up those stories to keep people out of their hunting area," said Johnny.

With Butch trotting behind him, Johnny put the back pack and his rifle in the trunk of his car. Butch jumped into the passenger seat when Johnny opened the door. Butch loved to ride in a vehicle where he could observe places away from the farm. Johnny turned on the car radio just in time to hear the weather forecast for the day. It was frosty outside with the temperature being twenty-eight degrees; it was supposed to warm up to around seventy degrees by noon. The sky was clear and the sun was beginning to rise with a golden glow through the trees.

Leaving the farm, there was a small herd of deer eating the new buds of grass in a field. They all looked up as Johnny's car went by, flicked their tails a few times and then went back to eating. It was ten miles to the gravel road where Johnny would park his car. Then there would be about a four mile hike along an old abandoned railroad grade. From there it would be a downhill walk into the remote forest, along the banks of a small stream. Butch was excited and couldn't wait to get out of the car. Outside of the car Butch scurried around smelling the air and the ground for any new scents.

It was still cool, but walking with a backpack and rifle soon made Johnny feel warm. "Okay, Butch, stay close and warn me of any other animals," said Johnny. The bears were now out of hibernation; mother bears would be close to their new cubs and very protective. The chances of running into a mountain lion, or a pack of wolves was farfetched, thought Johnny.

Reaching the small stream, coming out of the forest, Johnny and Butch stopped for a break. It was still morning and the sun was out, sending its warm rays to the earth. Johnny had a drink of water out of his canteen, while Butch dashed to the stream for a drink. A muskrat was on the bank of the river and stared at Butch with keen interest, as he approached. Butch, having had his drink, ran back to Johnny for a snack of some summer sausage. The muskrat figured Butch was no threat and continued his foraging. Johnny got out his camera and hung it around his neck; the camera was set and ready to take pictures. It had a zoom lens for close-ups at a distance, so as not to disturb whatever was being photographed.

After the short break, Johnny said to Butch," Stay close and watch out for danger." As they started up the stream bank, walking was easy. Last year's vegetation was flat on the ground, having been pushed down by the winter's snow. There were still patches of snow where the sun's exposure was limited. Walking upstream for a couple of miles, Johnny began to see signs of beaver. There were old beaver chewings of limbs and small trees had floated down the stream. There were no signs of any recent chewings, so these signs may have come from abandoned dams. This was what Johnny was looking for, so he could study the old dams and beaver houses.

After another half hour of walking, the stream opened up into a wide valley. It was treeless and large, abandoned dams came into view. The banks of the river had been steep, up to this point. Now, it was flat, wide open, and very different than the last few miles along the stream. Johnny understood why hunters would have to use helicopters to lift out any large game; it would be almost impossible to negotiate the steep hills. Johnny was tired from climbing the steep inclines and decided to take a rest on the side of a stream. There was still a thin sheet of ice around the edge of the dams, but there was open water in the middle. There was a very large beaver house, about twenty feet from the shore, in the first dam. This was perfect for Johnny; an abandoned dam and beaver house to study and photograph.

The dam was still in good shape and there were no recent beaver signs around it. The beavers either moved upstream, or to another stream, in search of food. Studying the dam, Johnny thought the beavers had first wedged longer poles into the soft stream bottom. Then they secured these poles with rocks to hold them in place. With spaces between the poles, branches were woven between these poles to form a net. More poles were pushed into this net to make it sturdier. Mud was then pushed up from the bottom to limit the amount of water running through the poles and branches. This would force the water to go over the top of the dam. More poles would be stuck in the pushed up mud to further strengthen the dam. Additional mud and rock would be pushed up to secure the new poles. Wherever a leak was happening, new branches would be used to plug the hole. This was a guess and Johnny would have to watch beavers building a dam to be sure. Summer would be the best time to observe this process, as the water in the streams would be at a lower level.

The construction of beaver houses was a mystery and to be sure, watching beavers build a house would be necessary to confirm Johnny's theory. Taking apart a beaver house would be an almost impossible task. Johnny and Butch crossed the dam walking on the beavers' chewed poles. The dam was still very firm and it would take years for the water to erode it. The dam provided wildlife a place to rest such as ducks and geese. Further scouting was needed to find the beavers' new territory.

Crossing over the dam and up the next steep, long bank of the stream, the hilltop became level. Johnny thought that beavers wouldn't climb up into the forest where predators roamed; they would stay near water. A predator would be wary of a beaver in the water. Beavers were capable of holding their breath for several minutes and could drown a predator, while holding it underwater.

Deciding to go back to the stream, the walk down the hill was much easier than going up. Johnny followed the water upstream and looked for new chewings; maybe from a small stream which fed into this main stream. Sure enough, Johnny's hunch was right. A few chewed branches had flowed out of a small creek coming out of another deep ravine "Okay, Butch, let's follow this little creek and find those beavers," said Johnny. Butch's ears shot straight up, he wagged his tail, and barked, as though he understood. There wasn't much bank along this little stream and fallen trees made it difficult to walk. After an hour of struggling through the narrow ravine, it opened up into a small valley. Staring straight ahead, Johnny could see a stand of aspen which was the favorite food of most beavers. Fresh chewings and downed aspen trees could be seen in the distance. Approaching the area where the new dam was under construction, Butch started barking at something under one of the fallen trees. When Johnny got closer, he could see that it was a beaver that had been pinned underneath a fallen tree. Sometimes a shift in the wind causes a tree which is to be felled toward the dam, to spin and change directions. It looked like this very thing had happened to this poor beaver. The beaver appeared to be dead, so Johnny decided to bury it.

Being wedged under the tree, Johnny would have to use a long pole to pry the tree off the beaver. Johnny told Butch, "When I tell you to pull, grab the beaver by the tail and pull him out." Butch sniffed the beaver a few times and then grabbed him by the tail. Johnny pulled down on the long pole which had been placed on a large rock to pry up on the tree. The tree wouldn't budge, as it was still connected to the stump. Johnny got his hatchet out of his pack and chopped the tree free from the stump. This time, the tree moved up a few inches and Butch was able to pull the beaver out. The beaver was bigger than Butch, but by using the strength of his four legs, he slid the beaver out. "Good job, Butch," said Johnny, as he approached the beaver. Johnny pulled it away from the stream and up a little embankment. Here, he would bury it. Johnny noticed two other beavers watching him from the bank of the stream. Johnny dug the grave, with his small folding shovel, for the unfortunate beaver. He then rolled it into the hole. Johnny was getting ready to cover the beaver's body with dirt when Butch started to whimper. "What's wrong with you, boy," Johnny asked Butch? Butch was looking at the beaver and poking it with his nose. That's when Johnny saw that the beaver was still breathing and had opened his eyes. Butch was able to sense that the beaver was not dead. Johnny pulled the beaver out of the hole and slid it back down to the edge of the stream. Johnny and Butch went back onto the embankment and watched as the two observing beavers approached the injured beaver. The beavers then did a strange thing. They covered the injured beaver on the bank with fresh aspen branches. Covering the beaver would give it some protection from predators and it could eat the bark off the branches which was their main source of food. This way, the injured beaver would have a chance to recover. Johnny thought what he had just witnessed, in the wild, was one of the most touching things he had ever seen.

The beaver house was in the process of being built. Short poles had been stuck into the dirt in a circular pattern about ten feet in diameter. Branches were woven between the poles' short chewings and mud was placed in the center. It was built up higher than the level of where the water would be in the dam. An opening on one side would allow the beavers to go underwater and come up to the raised area above the water. Long poles stuck into the outside of the raised area and came together at the top, like a teepee. Johnny took pictures of the beaver house before it was completed; now knew how these beavers made a house. The dam was not completed and was being built in separate sections. There was an opening on each end of the dam and one in the middle. Johnny noticed that large, thick pieces of the trees were near the edges of the dam.

These large pieces would be used to secure the openings when it came time to close the dam. When the dam was completed, the beaver house would be surrounded by water with an underwater entrance. The inside of the house would be warm and dry winter or summer. With ice freezing over the dam in the winter months, the beavers could leave their house underwater to gather food from the bottom of the dam. The wood for the building of the beaver house and the dam was the cast off wood left after the beavers had eaten off the bark. Additional wood with the bark still left on, was deposited in the bottom of the dam for winter food. The beavers would leave the house, pick up a piece of wood from the bottom of the dam, take it into the beaver house, and eat the bark. Eating the bark off the wood, the pole would then be placed in the bottom of the dam and used for repairs in the spring.

It was afternoon when Johnny and Butch started back toward the car. Before leaving, Johnny checked on the beaver he had thought was dead and had left at the edge of the stream. The same beaver was still there, munching on the aspen branches his beaver buddies had left for him. He glanced up at Johnny, and then went back to eating bark.

Getting back to the abandoned dam, Johnny was walking across it when he heard a loud scream. It was the unmistakable scream of a mountain lion, that wasn't showing any fear of Johnny or Butch. Even though Butch was barking as loud and ferocious as he could, the mountain lion began to cross the dam from the other side. Johnny swung his rifle up into firing position, hoping the mountain lion would retreat. Johnny fired a warning shot over the predator's head, but it still didn't stop coming toward him. Johnny sensed there was something wrong with this animal; maybe rabies. Johnny took another bead on the lion and was about to fire when he slipped and fell into the icy water of the dam. The rifle slipped from his hands. Butch had leaped into the dam to escape the mountain lion as well. Johnny swam toward the beaver house, hoping the mountain lion wouldn't come after him. Butch was on top of the beaver house barking; he would be no match for the mountain lion. The mountain lion leaped into the dam and started to swim toward Johnny. Johnny had one chance and that would be to find the entrance to the beaver house. Butch had come down to the edge of the beaver house still barking and growling. Johnny grabbed Butch and dove under the water looking for the entrance to the beaver house. He couldn't find it and had to come up for air. Butch was struggling and thought he was drowning. Reaching the surface for more air, Johnny came almost face-to-face with the mountain lion. Pulling Butch under the water with him again, Johnny found the entrance to the beaver house.

Johnny pushed Butch up and inside the beaver house, then squeezed through the entrance himself. Inside the beaver house, they would be safe from the mountain lion. Johnny was cold and was thinking about hypothermia. Butch would be okay because he had his thick coat of fur. Johnny took off his jacket, shirt, and long underwear top, wrung them as dry as he could and put them back on himself. Then, the boots, pants, long underwear bottoms and socks were wrung out and put back on as well. Johnny and Butch shivered from the cold. After about an hour, it had become comfortable inside the beaver house. It was dark inside the house except for an air hole at the top where the mountain lion was clawing to get in. Johnny knew it was fruitless for the mountain lion to gain entrance from the top because the beavers had built their house too strong to allow any predator to enter uninvited. With the evening coming on, Johnny decided to spend the night in the beaver house and go out the next morning after the sun had risen.

Johnny's back pack and rifle were somewhere in the dam and he would have to find them before leaving. When he could see light through the air hole, he knew it was time to go. Butch didn't want to go back in that cold water, but Johnny pushed him through the hole underwater and he popped up like a cork in the dam. When Johnny came out, the mountain lion was nowhere to be seen.

"Cold water wakes you up," said Johnny to Butch. Johnny could see his rifle and backpack, under the water, near the edge of the dam. After recovering them, Johnny figured that he and Butch would be okay walking back to the car in the warm sunshine. The car was about three hours away and the walk felt good. Butch shook himself dry along the way. Reaching the car, Johnny took off his pack and just lay back in the sun. Butch was tuckered out and was sprawled out on the front seat with his eyes closed. The camera and film had been put in a sealed plastic bag, so the pictures should turn out well.

CHAPTER 10
SKIING WITH HUNGRY WOLVES

Winters in the Upper Peninsula of Michigan could be quite severe and even brutal. All that separated this area from Canada was Lake Superior. Sometimes it snowed so much that the county plows weren't able to push it all off the roads. It wasn't unusual to be snow-bound on the farm for three or four days after a snowstorm. The way to clear the roads was with a huge new machine; it could gobble up the snow in its large, rotating blades and throw it through the air for fifty feet or more. The machine moved at a slow rate of about ten miles per hour.

When the snow banks became high enough, some of the local boys, including Johnny, would ski on top of them. Pulled behind a car on a long rope, the boys on skis would climb the high snow banks and ski along the top of the banks. It was like water skiing, except on snow. Unlike water skiing, there were obstacles to maneuver around, such as small trees and mailboxes. The skier would flip the rope over the top of the mailbox, or tree, and continue skiing.

Sometimes, the rope would not clear the obstacle and the skier would have to let go of the rope and maybe go tumbling head-over-heels in the snow. It was a little bit dangerous, but great fun on a nice, clear, sunny day. Speeds up to thirty or forty miles per hour could be attained, so watching for obstacles was important. At crossroads, one would have to ski down the bank to the road. Once past the intersection, one could ski up the bank again and continue the fun. Some skiers would have the driver speed up the car to try and jump across the intersection in the air; however, most of the time, they were unsuccessful. The forestry roads were the best places to ski the banks, as they were wide and with no mailboxes to worry about.

Johnny went over to Sam's farm and asked him if he wanted to go skiing behind the car. "Sure, said Sam; it's nice out." "I'll pull you first," said Johnny, as he hooked a rope to the bumper of his car. Out onto the forestry roads the boys went with Sam enjoying skiing on the wide banks. There weren't any crossroads to worry about; however, there were creeks running across the road in places. Although frozen, the snow banks of the creeks were too deep to navigate. Coming to a creek, the skier would have to pull back onto the main road. Sam hollered, "Speed it up so I can jump over the next creek." Johnny said, "Okay, I hope you can make it, as he increased the speed of the car. At the bank of the creek, Sam raised his skis into the air and hoped to land on the other bank.

After Johnny passed the creek, Sam didn't appear on the other bank and a dangling, empty rope trailed behind the car. What happened to Sam, thought Johnny? Stopping the car, Johnny ran back to the creek to check on Sam. "Sam, are you okay," asked Johnny? "Yes, just full of snow from my tumble," said Sam. "I didn't clear the other bank. My my ski tips stuck in the snow and I went flying through the air," said Sam. "It's a good thing snow is soft and you didn't break anything," said Johnny. "It's my turn to ski on the way back, but I'm not going to try jumping any creeks," said Johnny. Turning the car around, Johnny skied back to Sam's farm.

Downhill skiing in the country was fun, but the walk back up the hill to make another run was hard and tiring. There were some long, steep hills to be found in the farm country. Some neighbor boys would come over to Johnny's farm to ski the big hill. "Let's make a ski jump," said one of the boys. "Great idea," said Johnny. "Let's make it halfway down the hill." Using snow the boys packed a jump about five feet high. "Let's see how far we can fly," said one of the neighbor boys. The first boy down took a tumble on landing. Then it was Johnny's turn. "Here I come," said Johnny, as he headed for the jump. Pushing off the end of the jump, Johnny sailed through the air for about forty feet, landing upright and exhilarated. "That was fun," said Johnny. "Maybe we can build the jump higher next time," said Sam. The boys enjoyed the ski jumping for a while. Then one of the boys said, "Let's go off the ski jump on a toboggan." All the boys piled on the long toboggan. Sailing through the air on the toboggan was exciting until they landed. When the toboggan landed, it was with a thud which jarred the passengers. "No more going off the ski jump on a toboggan. Its fun until you land," the boys exclaimed!

A dam had been built on a little creek to water the cattle during the summer. Now, in the middle of winter, it was frozen and could be used for ice skating. The snow had to be shoveled off the ice and the ice flooded with water to re-freeze for a smooth surface. Johnny's brothers and sisters had skates, but Johnny didn't have any. After the snow was cleared from the ice, several other neighbor kids came over to join in the fun. Johnny decided to use his sleigh on the ice. With a running start, he would then jump on the sleigh, careening across the pond. It was all going well until Johnny hit a tree stump underneath the snow on the opposite bank. The sleigh stopped and Johnny flew forward over the sleigh, ramming his head into the stump. When Johnny got up, his head was lying on his shoulder and he thought he had broken his neck. He didn't want the others to know about his condition, so he walked across the ice and went home. When he got home, his mother asked him why he was laying his head on his shoulder.

Johnny said, "I hit a stump with my sleigh, my head fell down on my shoulder, and I can't move it," said Johnny. "You could have a broken neck. Don't try and move your head; we're going to see a doctor right now," said his mother.

Upon arriving at Dr. Bender's office, he looked at Johnny in a peculiar way, saying, "What happened to you?" Johnny said, "I hit a stump underneath the snow with my sleigh and my head rammed the stump, as I flew forward." "We will have to x-ray your neck to look for a fracture," said Dr. Bender. The x-rays didn't show a fracture; however, the neck vertebrae were out of place. Dr. Bender called Dr. Henderson, a Chiropractor, to put Johnny's neck back in place. Dr. Henderson said he had never seen a misalignment this severe, without a fracture. "Lie down on this examining table, and relax," said Dr. Henderson. He pulled Johnny's head up and gave it a quick twist. It was a little frightening to Johnny when he heard something snap in his neck, but it didn't hurt. "Sit up," said Dr. Henderson to Johnny. When Johnny sat up, his head was straight up and not lying on his shoulder anymore. Johnny exclaimed, "Wow, I'm okay again!" "Thanks, doctor." After they left the doctor's office, Johnny's mother took him to Johnson's Drug Store for a juicy cheeseburger, fries and chocolate malt. They sat together at the soda fountain, on red swivel stools and discussed how relieved they were that Johnny's accident had not been crippling, or fatal. He thought to himself how wonderful his mother was and how much he loved her. Johnny decided, in his mind, that sleighing on frozen ponds was not a good idea.

Cross country ski racing was exciting to people of all ages in Upper Peninsula, Michigan. It was great fun and togetherness; in fact, as soon as kids could walk, they were fitted with little skis and off they went like ducks to water! Every year, the most exciting race was the open category with no age limit. However, this was one race that few of the most advanced and fittest skiers could finish.

Johnny, being in great athletic condition, decided to enter the race; he thought that maybe he could win a nice prize. There were many excellent skiers in the area, so the competition was great. The bragging rights seemed to be more important than the prizes. It was a long, grueling race that lasted three days. The start of the race began at seven o'clock in the morning and finished each day by five o'clock p.m. There were many checkpoints along the trail, so it was impossible to cheat in this race. The person who reached the most checkpoints would be declared the winner. Stops were made as often as each skier wanted. Refreshments and food were served along the trail for the skiers.

Wolves posed the greatest threat along the ski trail. If the wolves were getting plenty of food, they were no threat; however, if they were hungry, they ran in packs, hunting food and could be quite dangerous to the skiers. The snow was deep this winter so it was hard for the wolves to catch their usual prey. Some skiers carried pistols for protection but Johnny didn't own one.

This year's winner of the race would receive a new red pickup truck. The race was over three days. It started with around five hundred skiers and ended up with less than one hundred finishing. Falls, sprains and cold weather conditions were the usual causes for most of the skiers to drop out. The first day was sunny and crisp with no wind; a perfect day for cross-country skiing. Some of the contestants had fancy store-bought skis, boots and ski gear; however, Johnny had homemade skis made out of Aspen. They were long, but light in weight. They didn't have bindings; instead, a leather strap was placed across the toes.

Most people had special waxes for their skis but Johnny's father had prepared his skis in a special way. Johnny's father had warmed up some pine tar on the stove then painted the entire ski with the tar. Once the tar had cooled, he poured alcohol in a coffee can and lit it on fire. He ran the skis over the fire and wiped off the excess melted tar. He continued this process until the cloth came out clean. The skis looked stripped with a tan and brown color to them. Johnny's father said, "Okay, go outside and try them." Johnny took the skis outside and slipped his toes under the straps. The snow would not stick to the skis and Johnny almost fell down because the skis were so slippery. Johnny went out across a field and couldn't believe how easy it was to slide the skis across the snow. It was a trick his father had learned from the men who drove the horse-drawn sleighs in the lumber camps. The men would use this procedure on the sleighs that hauled the heavy logs. With the special pine tar treatment used on the blades of the large sleighs, the horses had no trouble pulling the logging sleighs through the snow.

With entry numbers pined to the backs and fronts of their jackets, the contestants would be staggered at two minute intervals when starting the race. Everyone was provided with a whistle, on a chain, around their necks, to blow in case they got into trouble. With the increased wolf population in the area, rangers were going to patrol the course by snow mobile. The trails went across lakes where the wind could become a factor. The easiest part of the course would be through the flat, forested area away from the wind and the steep hills. The course covered one hundred twenty miles through all kinds of terrain. Johnny thought he was in good enough condition to finish the race, even though it would be exhausting.

The race started on time and Johnny was third in line at the starting gate. His skis were very slippery which made the start of the race easy and smooth. After about thirty minutes into the race, Johnny flew by some of the contestants who had started before him. As far as he could tell, there was one other skier ahead of him. There were two ski trails parallel to each other, so two skiers were sent off together. As Johnny came near a frozen lake, he knew he could pass the skier in front of him, as his skis flew across the snow. Johnny thought to himself, my father knew what he was doing to make these skis slide so fast. Johnny was now in the lead and was making good time. Wouldn't it be something if I could win that new pickup truck, thought Johnny? After about an hour and a half, Johnny was out of sight of the skiers closest behind him.

Johnny came to his third checkpoint. Hot coffee, tea and energy snacks were free to the contestants and he enjoyed them. He couldn't afford the time to linger for very long, as he didn't want the skiers behind him to have a chance to catch up to him. There would be a checkpoint about every five miles through the mountains. The trail was becoming more difficult, as Johnny skied up and down the steep hills. It was easy coming down and so much work trying to get up the hills with his homemade, slippery skis. The time he gained going down the hills was lost as he struggled to get up the hills. The checkpoints were welcome stops going through the mountains, even though the stops were a minute or less. Johnny's legs were aching from climbing those steep foothills of the mountains. Reaching the flat forest area was a relief, even though there were no hills to ski down. The trail through the forest passed by large virgin pine, spruce and cedar; these trees were tall, wide, and had been bypassed by the Lumberjacks of long ago.

Johnny felt like something was watching him, but couldn't see anything out of the ordinary. Just then, he heard the howls of wolves behind him. He thought they were chasing rabbits or maybe a deer, but when he looked back, they were following him. Johnny wished he had a pistol with him right now. The wolves were a couple hundred yards behind him, but were gaining ground each time he went up a hill. As a rule, wolves didn't bother people, but maybe they were hungry. Johnny was trying to out ski them, but knew the next checkpoint was too far away; the wolves would catch him before he got there. Johnny thought he would have to leave the trail and ski off a cliff to lose the wolves. He figured the wolves would then quit the pursuit and he would be safe. Johnny's heart was beating fast, as he was giving it all he had to outrun the wolves. The wolves were now about seventy-five yards behind him and gaining. He could see a cliff about two hundred yards ahead and thought this was his best chance. Johnny got off the trail and headed for the cliff. With the wolves ten yards behind him, Johnny flew off the cliff like an Olympic ski jumper. Sailing through the air and hoping to land on his skis, he looked for a good landing spot. He hit the downhill slope about seventy-five feet below the cliff. The snow was soft and Johnny's skis sank in too deep; he went tumbling through the snow. He sat up and appeared to be unhurt. The wolves looked down at him from the ridge of the cliff. They were whining and howling but not about to leap off the cliff.

Then, Johnny heard the crack of a rifle shot and the wolves disappeared from the cliff, as a ranger on a snowmobile appeared and hollered, "Are you alright?" Johnny hollered back, "Yes, I'm okay, thanks for coming by." "Stay where you are and I'll come and get you," yelled the ranger. Johnny could hear the high-pitched sound of the snowmobile making its way down the mountain to where he was. When the ranger arrived, he said, "It's unusual for wolves to follow a person, so you were very lucky." Johnny's skis were okay, but he was out of the race and would not win the shiny new truck for his father. The ranger gave Johnny a ride to the next checkpoint station where he warmed up with hot cocoa. Oh well, he thought, there was always next year.

Johnny thought about the coming summer when he and Sam would be looking for a certain shipwreck in Lake Superior that was rumored to have a chest full of twenty dollar gold coins.

CHAPTER 11
SUNKEN TREASURE

One evening Johnny and Sam were sitting around, discussing treasure stories they had heard and wondered if any of them were true. "Sam, do you remember a couple of years ago when we sawed and chopped firewood for that old man, down on Green River," asked Johnny? "I remember him. That was Crazy Charlie O'Casey," said Sam. He said he would tell us a true treasure tale that he had never told anyone else, if we would help him make five cords of firewood," said Sam. We thought it was a tall tale made up in the mind of Crazy Charlie," said Johnny. "I was reading a book, on the history of this area, to get information to write a book report for History class at school," said Johnny. "There was an incident in this book which sounded like the story Crazy Charlie told us," said Johnny. Crazy Charlie said, "Boys, this is a true treasure tale as told to me by my father."

"Back in the 1850's, my father was a cabin boy on a sailing ship that hauled cargo on the Great Lakes," said Charlie. The ship stopped at a port on Lake Superior to pick up cargo and passengers for the trip to Copper Harbor. The destination was on Upper Michigan's Keweenaw Peninsula. The passengers who boarded the ship were a group of rough looking characters who carried two large chests onto the ship. The chests seemed to be very heavy, as it took four men to carry each of them. Soon after the ship left port, the rough looking men took control of the ship. When the ship was about one mile from shore, the same rough looking men killed the crew and dumped their bodies overboard. When it came to the young cabin boy, none of the scoundrels wanted to shoot a boy so they just threw him into the lake's cold, icy water. The men figured the boy would soon become numb from the icy water and drown. What they didn't know was that Charlie's father was a strong swimmer who often swam in the cold water of the lake. When Charlie's father landed in the water, he pretended that he couldn't swim very well and the men laughed at his attempts. Once out of sight of the men on the ship, he started to swim toward the shore. The water was cold and he knew he could not stop. If he stopped swimming the freezing water would have slowed his movements and he would have drowned. The shore seemed a long way away, but he had youth and determination on his side. He had been in the water for over an hour when he reached the shore and collapsed on the warm sand. After lying on the beach for a few minutes, he decided to walk toward a lighthouse in the distance.

His muscles were so tired from swimming that he stopped several times to rest before reaching the lighthouse. He didn't know where he was but had heard the lighthouse's fog horn up the beach and hoped it was being manned. Upon reaching the lighthouse, he tried to open the door, but it was locked; maybe the lighthouse keeper would return in the evening. Charlie's father leaned against the door and fell asleep. He was awakened by the lighthouse keeper who had returned and was wondering what a boy was doing in such a deserted area. "What are you doing here," the lighthouse keeper asked?

Charlie's father told his story to the lighthouse keeper who was amazed that a boy so young could have swum a mile in the freezing water. "We have to go to the authorities in Calumet. They are the law enforcement around here. It's about ten miles; I'll ride my horse and you can ride my pack mule. We have to tell them what happened," said the lighthouse keeper."

Arriving in Calumet, the lighthouse keeper relayed the story to the fort commander.

The fort commander told the lighthouse keeper that an army patrol was escorting two chests of gold and silver coins from Chicago to Calumet, for a rich banking family, when they were ambushed and killed. The fort commander sent a patrol along the shoreline of Lake Superior to search for the sailing ship. "When we catch those murdering thieves, they will all hang for what they have done," said the fort commander.

The patrol spotted a burning ship about a mile offshore and reported it to the fort commander. The thieves had set fire to the ship to hide their whereabouts. They loaded the chests into the life boats and rowed back to shore. Then they rowed up a large river to a small stream which led to a small lake. They went out into the lake and lowered the chests into about twenty feet of water. Ropes were attached to the handles of the chests so that the chests could be retrieved at a later date. The ropes were tied to the roots of a large oak tree near the water. The ropes were buried and covered with sand to hide them. One thief, who was sick, stayed at the lake to guard the chests. He was given food to last about three weeks when the other thieves would be back to claim their treasure. The thieves' plan was to row back to the big lake and hide out until they were sure that no one suspected them of their evil deeds.

Charlie's father had no home to go back to, so the lighthouse keeper said he could stay with him until he found a job. He found work with a lumber company helping the cook prepare food for the Lumberjacks. Meanwhile, the soldiers, patrolling the area, spotted the thieves rowing the life boats down a large river, back toward the big lake and town. About a mile from town, the thieves sunk the life boats in the river and came ashore. The soldiers were waiting in the nearby woods and captured the thieves once they were on land. The thieves were brought to Fort Henry and imprisoned. A trial was held and the thieves were found guilty. Their sentence was to hang for the killing of the soldiers. The thieves tried to bargain out of their sentence, using the chests of coins as a bargaining tool. It didn't do any good and the thieves were hung without telling the location of the chests.

One day, Charlie's father was sent into town from the lumber camp with a wagon to buy supplies for the cook shack. While in the general store, Charlie's father spotted one of the thieves across the street from the store. The thief, who had been left behind, had seen Charlie's father go into the store and had recognized him as the cabin boy they had thrown into the lake. The thief had come into town when his food ran out to look for his associates. Arriving in town, he found out that his accomplices had been captured, tried, and hung.

The thief had taken a job, in town, cleaning a saloon to survive. He was the lone person who knew where the coins were hidden. He couldn't tell anybody about the chests, as he would be sure to hang like his partners in crime. The thief was in poor health and needed some of those coins to get medical assistance. He borrowed a horse from the saloon owner and rode back to the lake. At the lake, the thief hooked the horse up to one of the strong ropes. He was leading the horse, trying to pull one of the chests to shore, when the rope went slack. When he pulled the rope in, a handle of one of the chests was at the end. The same thing happened to the other three ropes. He had the handles of the chests, but no chests. The chests had sunken into the sand and couldn't be pulled ashore by the handles. The chests needed to be pulled up from the sand from a boat. The thief came back to town empty handed.

The thief waited for Charlie's father to come out of the store. Charlie's father wanted to turn the thief in to the authorities, but there wasn't any law enforcement in town. When Charlie's father got to his wagon, the thief was waiting for him. Charlie's father, speaking in a mean, low voice said, "What do you want?" Charlie's father was thinking the worst, but the thief surprised him by asking for his help. The culprit told Charlie's father that if he would give him a backpack full of supplies and twenty dollars, he would tell him the location of the chests. Not trusting the intentions of the thief, Charlie's father was skeptical, but nodded in agreement.

Charlie's father insisted that the thief draw him a map of the exact location of the chests. "I can give you the supplies you want, and I have ten dollars in silver coins," said Charlie's father." The thief said he would accept the supplies and the silver coins in exchange for the map with the location of the chests. The thief drew the map and handed it to Charlie's father. Charlie's father gave him the provisions and ten dollars in silver coins; the thief left town. Charlie's father planned to go to Calumet and tell the fort commander about the thief. He thought he might get a reward if the thief was captured.

It had been three months since the robbery had taken place and this was Charlie's father's first trip into town from the logging camp. He went back into the store to get directions to Calumet from the clerk. The clerk told him the fort in Calumet had burned down a month ago and the soldiers had been reassigned to other forts. With no one in law enforcement to tell, Charlie's father kept the secret and the map to himself.

It was spring break-up at the lumber camp and Charlie's father decided that he would go look for the lake with the treasure chests in its waters. The thief said the treasure chests were in about twenty feet of water and the spot was marked by the four ropes hanging from the oak tree. Riding a horse and following the directions on the map, Charlie's father found the lake. There was a stream exiting the lake which the thieves must have used to row the treasure chests to the lake. Close to where the stream left the lake, Charlie's father spotted the oak tree with the ropes hanging from one of its limbs. The big problem was how to hook onto the chests. He tried grappling hooks, scoops and several other devices, but nothing he tried could move those chests. He didn't dare get anybody else involved in the chests' recovery, as he didn't know anyone he could trust. He couldn't go to the authorities, since they would have asked him why he hadn't reported it earlier. He thought they might even think he had been involved with the thieves.

Charlie's father had to make a living, so he went to work in a blacksmith shop. He fell in love with the blacksmith's daughter and got married. Soon after, Charlie was born. Charlie was doing fine as a kid until one day he got kicked in the head by his father's horse. Charlie's senses were never normal again; that's why people called him, "Crazy" Charlie. When Charlie was older, his father sat him down and told him the story about the treasure chests in the lake and gave him a map showing the location. Charlie understood what his father had told him, but thought he would never be able to recover the treasure chests.

Charlie was afraid to tell anyone the story that his father had told him. People thought he was crazy already and he didn't want them to put him in a mental institution. He lived alone in a tar paper shack, on the outskirts of town. He survived by trapping and doing odd jobs for people. Charlie's father told him not to tell anyone about the map he had given him. Charlie hid the map in his cabin but couldn't remember where. He did tell the boys the name of the lake and said if they could find an old oak tree with ropes hanging from one of its limbs, they should be able to locate the treasure.

"I know where that lake is. Maybe we should check it out; it's about a mile up a stream off the big river. Let's plan on going there next weekend," said Sam. "If the chests are in twenty feet of water, we will need scuba gear to get to them," said Johnny. "I know a man who does scuba diving; maybe we could borrow his equipment. We would have to take training and become certified before he would let us use his gear," said Sam. "Where can we get training," asked Johnny? "The YMCA has classes each summer and I think they start next week," said Sam. "Let's take the training," said Johnny. Sam said, "First we have to see if we can find the lake and the oak tree with the ropes. Why don't we go tomorrow? "I'll pick you up at seven o'clock in the morning," said Johnny.

Johnny was awake at sunup the next morning. He ate a big pancake and bacon breakfast, did some chores, and was ready to go. He told his mother that he and Sam were going on a canoe trip and would be back before dark. "Okay. Take a gun and some food with you," said Johnny's mother. "I have everything I need in my backpack," said Johnny. He hugged his mother goodbye and told her where they were going. Then he jumped in his car and sped off down the dusty, red dirt road, to Sam's farm.

Sam had been up for a long time, milking the cows and working in the barn. He had just put the cows out in the pasture to graze when Johnny arrived. Sam had already gotten the canoe out of the barn and had it sitting alongside the driveway. The boys tied it to the top of Johnny's car. With the canoe secured to the top of the car and packs in the back seat, the boys took off down the road. Arriving at the river, the boys jumped out and untied the canoe. Putting the canoe in the water, the boys loaded the gun and backpacks in it, securing them with nylon straps. With life preservers on, the boys started paddling up the big river. It would be a ten mile trek up the river to reach the small stream. Arriving at the small stream, the boys took a break. Paddling upstream for ten miles was tiring. At the stream to the lake, the boys rowed the canoe upstream having to carry it around trees that had fallen into the stream. It didn't take long for the boys to arrive at the lake." "Charlie said the oak tree with the ropes was close to the stream exiting the lake," said Johnny. "I don't see any oak trees near the water. Do you think he told us a tall tale," asked Sam? "I don't know," said Johnny. "Maybe the tree died and fell into the lake near the shoreline," said Sam. About one hundred yards from the stream, the boys spotted a large tree that had fallen into the lake and was underwater. Can you see any ropes attached to the tree," asked Sam? "None that I can see," said Johnny. "Maybe a fisherman or trapper took the ropes. I think the tree in the water could be an oak," said Johnny. "Look! There's a piece of rotted rope wrapped around one of the decaying roots of the tree," said Sam. Sure enough, a piece of weathered, knotted rope was still clinging to the root of the tree. "The thief must have found it easier to cut the rope rather than untie the knots," said Sam. "I think we found our tree," said Johnny.

"Let's put the canoe in the lake and see if we can spot the chests," said Sam. The boys ran to the canoe and were giddy with excitement! Launching the canoe in the lake, the boys paddled to the sunken oak tree. Looking down in the clear water, there was no sign of any chests. "The heavy chests could have sunken into the lake bottom and could be covered up with silt," said Johnny. "Maybe somebody found them and retrieved them," said Sam. "Crazy Charlie said he never told anyone about the chests," said Johnny. "It's been over one hundred years that the chests have been on the bottom of the lake, so they could still be there," said Sam. "Let's go back and check on those scuba diving lessons at the YMCA," said Johnny. The boys paddled back to the stream and headed to town. It was a lot easier going back, as the current of the river pushed the boys downstream. When they got back to the car, they loaded the canoe and went straight to the YMCA.

The YMCA was open every day, so the boys got their information at the front desk. The scuba classes would start on Monday and last two weeks. It cost twenty dollars per person and the YMCA supplied the necessary equipment. Johnny and Sam filled out an application and signed up for the upcoming classes. They would be taking their lessons at the YMCA's indoor, heated twelve-foot deep pool. The lessons were from seven until nine, five nights per week. Once the tests were passed, at the end of the two weeks, a card was issued to the graduates allowing them to buy compressed air. Both a written test, as well as a hands-on test using the scuba equipment in the water was required. During the training, the boys were glad they had already taken swimming and lifeguard training a couple of years earlier. They had become good, strong swimmers which made swimming with the heavy air tanks much easier. The boys completed their scuba training and got their Certified Scuba Diver cards. Now they could purchase compressed air. The next day they would go visit Sam's friend, who had the scuba gear, to see if they could borrow the equipment from him.

The boys drove over to see Joe Busby, who was Sam's friend and his wife, Evelyn. Joe was outside pruning some apple trees when the boys arrived. Joe was a large man, six feet, four inches tall and close to three hundred pounds. He had long, white hair tied in a pony tail and a thick, bushy beard to match. "Howdy, boys, come on in the house and say hello to Evelyn," said Joe. Inside the house was like a museum with things Joe had found while scuba diving. Evelyn was in the kitchen and came to the living room to greet the boys. "This is my friend, Johnny," said Sam. "We're glad to meet you," said Joe and Evelyn. "Sam, tell us what you have been doing since we last saw you," said Joe. Sam said, "Johnny and I just completed the scuba training course at the YMCA and received our Certified Scuba Diver cards, so we can now buy compressed air. "That's great," said Joe. "Are you boys planning some scuba diving trips," asked Evelyn? "Yes, we want to dive in a local lake for practice. Our problem is that we don't have any scuba gear and we were wondering if you would loan us a set," said Sam. "Sure, we have several sets; you boys could use my wetsuit, as I don't dive anymore," said Evelyn. "I just baked a fresh apple pie with apples from our own trees. Would you like a piece with whipped cream," asked Evelyn? "Oh yes, that sounds wonderful," said Sam. Johnny's face lit up with approval as well. "Let's go to the table in the kitchen and sample it," said Joe. After having the pie and coffee, Johnny said, "That was delicious pie and I enjoyed every bite," said Johnny. Sam, likewise, expressed his appreciation for the unexpected hospitality. Joe said, "Let's go and find you some scuba gear."

"How deep will you be diving," asked Joe? "About twenty feet," said Sam. "It's safer if you dive together, so I'm going to give you two sets of scuba gear," said Joe. "I have one good wet suit of Evelyn's and one older suit that has a couple of small tears in it, but it will still work. I also have a compressor to fill the tanks," said Joe. The boys thanked Joe and left with the car full of scuba diving gear. The boys were so excited to have all this scuba gear and the chance to find sunken treasure in the lake. They laughed and talked all the way home, as they planned their first diving adventure.

"It's going to be tough paddling the canoe upriver with all the weight of the scuba gear," said Johnny. "We can always pull over to the bank of the river for a rest," said Sam. "You're right, we don't have to rush, to get up the river," said Johnny. "What we need is one of those underwater metal detectors," said Johnny. "That would be nice, but where could we get one," asked Sam? "They are for sale in the treasure magazines, but we can't afford to buy one," said Johnny. "I guess we will just have to use metal rods and poke around through the silt," said Sam. "Let's go to the lake next Saturday," said Johnny. "I'll get the metal rods and you get a pail and some oat feed sacks," said Johnny. "If we find the coins, we have to have something strong to carry then in and the burlap oat feed sacks will work just fine," said Sam. "We will also need a hammer, a chisel and a crowbar to break the locks. We would never be able to move the chests, as the wood could be rotted after having been in the lake for over one hundred years," said Sam.

Saturday came and the boys packed the car with the scuba gear and the other needed items. They headed for the big river with the canoe on top of the car. After unloading the canoe and packing it with their gear, they began an exhausting trip upriver. After several rest stops, they came to the stream that would take them to the lake. Carrying the canoe, coupled with the extra weight of the scuba gear around the fallen trees in the river was harder than they had anticipated. They arrived at the lake happy but tired. "We had better take a rest before going into the water," said Johnny. "I'm for that," said Sam, as he lay back on the lake shore and covered his eyes with his hat.

After a short rest, Johnny said, "Sam, it's time to go find treasure!" "Let's get our wet suits on and get in the lake," said Sam. The boys got all their scuba gear on and checked the air in their tanks. They were nervous because this was their first time to use scuba gear outside of the safe environment of the twelve-foot deep pool at the YMCA. This was the real thing! They entered the cold water of Crystal Lake, but it soon felt warmer in the wet suits. The water was clear and the sun was out so the boys didn't need any additional lighting. They swam out to where the lake was twenty feet deep and started probing with their long, metal rods.

The silt was three or four feet thick – just enough to hide the treasure chests. After twenty minutes of probing with no results, the boys came out of the water disappointed at not having found anything promising so far. The boys just sat on the beach staring out at the vast lake. Johnny said, "Sam, I was thinking about the level of the lake one hundred years ago. What if it were different back then? With the stream running out of the lake, the level could have been higher," said Sam. "You're right, Sam, the water flowing from the lake would have cut into the earth, thereby lowering the lake level," said Johnny. "We've been looking in too deep of water," said Sam. "Let's work our way in from the twenty foot depth toward the shore," said Johnny.

With newfound excitement, the boys went back into the lake with their probes. In ten feet of water, Sam struck something solid. He motioned Johnny over who stuck his probe in the silt near Sam and also hit the solid object two feet into the silt. The boys stuck their thumbs up to indicate they had found something. The boys went to shore to get the canoe paddles to clear away the silt. Excited, the boys were smiling, as they headed back into the water with the canoe paddles.

The boys removed their probes and started clearing away the silt with the paddles. The water became cloudy and they could feel the silt on the end of their paddles. When the boys had cleared away the two feet of silt, they backed off to let the water clear. When the water cleared, the boys saw the top of a large wooden chest. Then the boys cleared away some more silt and found the lock which held the lid down. They went back to the canoe to get the hammer, chisel and a crowbar. With the tools in hand, the boys headed back into the water. They tried breaking the lock open with the crowbar, but it was corroded shut and wouldn't open. Next, they tried the hammer and chisel, but in the water, the hammer couldn't be swung with enough force to do much good. What the boys needed was a hacksaw to cut off the lock.

I have a hacksaw in my toolbox in the car," said Johnny. "We had better refill our tanks with air. Mine is almost empty," said Sam. "Let's stow our stuff up in the woods out of sight, until we get back," said Johnny. The boys retrieved the canoe paddles from the lake and put the air tanks in the canoe. They changed back into their dry clothes and headed back. It was easy going back downstream and the boys didn't have to make any stops. They were in an elated mood and had discussed their good fortune all the way down the river. It was now late in the afternoon and the boys would have to wait until tomorrow to go back to the lake. They headed straight over to Joe's to get the tanks refilled. Joe was home and filled the tanks for the boys and asked if they were having fun. The boys assured Joe that they were indeed enjoying themselves. On the way home, it began to rain big, hard drops. There were black clouds forming overhead. Sam said, "It looks like a storm brewing in the direction of the river. We will have to wait for this bad weather to blow over before we can paddle back up the river."

"We might have to wait a couple of days," replied Johnny. "The river might be raging and sending trees and debris in its currents." The storm lasted through the night and all the next day. The river was running fast and furious, so the boys had to wait two days before attempting to paddle up river.

The boys were restless and couldn't wait any longer to get back to their secret treasure operation. They paddled up the river with just a few stops to rest. The storm had knocked more trees down on the small stream, so more carrying the canoe was involved. At the lake, the boys rested before getting the belongings from the woods. Back into their wet suits, with their air tanks strapped to their backs, and hacksaw in hand, the boys entered the water with much anticipation.

The storm had no effect on the lake and the chest was still uncovered just like they had left it. Johnny reached down for the lock and started sawing with the hacksaw. The hacksaw was able to cut the rusty hasp and Johnny removed the lock. The boys tried lifting the lid but it wouldn't open. Sam used the crowbar to pry off the lid and it popped open. Inside the chest were several sacks with something in them. Sam reached in and grabbed the top sack which ripped open, spilling large silver coins into the chest. The boys had found the chest full of silver coins! Then they reached down into the chest and grabbed a handful of coins. It was hard to contain themselves in ten feet of water! They were breathless with excitement over their find!

The boys went back to shore to see what kind of coins they had recovered. They were jumping up and down and hugging each other when they noticed that the coins in their hands were silver dollars. "Wow, we have found something this time," exclaimed Johnny! I wonder what is in those other sacks," said Sam. "I don't know, but we will find out soon," said Johnny. "Let's get the pail and start hauling those coins out of the water and put them in the burlap sacks," said Sam. It took about an hour to remove all the coins from the chest. There were silver dollars, half dollars, quarters, dimes and nickels. The boys estimated that there was at least five thousand dollars or more.

"We have to bury the coins in the woods and take a couple of sacks with us," said Johnny. The coins were in rotted sacks in the chest, so the strong burlap oat sacks were used to hold the coins. "We don't have a shovel, so we have to hide the coins in the woods," said Sam. The boys went into the woods to look for a place to hide the sacks of coins. They found a hollowed out pine log a couple hundred yards into the woods. "This is a perfect place to hide the coins," said Johnny. The boys counted their steps back to the lake. Johnny said, "I counted two hundred and eight-seven paces to the lake." Sam said, "I counted two hundred and eighty four." "Let's get the coins and put them in the hollow log," said Sam. The boys carried six sacks of coins to the hollow log and covered everything with brush. The log was in a direct line between the oak tree in the water and a rock outcropping at the top of the hill. With two sacks of coins and the scuba tanks, the boys headed back to the car. The river was still full of trees and branches left by the storm, even though the water level had gone down.

On the way downstream, the canoe hit one of the trees under the surface of the muddy water. It tore a hole in the canoe and water started to gush inside. Sam took off his life jacket and tied it to one of the sacks of coins." Then he jumped out of the canoe into the murky water of the river. Sam hollered, "Johnny, tie your life jacket to the other sack of coins." With water gushing into the canoe, Johnny tied his life jacket to the other sack of coins. "Throw the coin sacks into the water," yelled Sam. Johnny threw the coin sacks overboard attached to the life jackets. With the canoe lighter, Johnny was able to paddle close to the shore before it sank. With one end of the canoe sticking out of the water, Johnny swam to shore. Johnny was hoping that the scuba tanks were still in the canoe. Where was Sam, thought Johnny? He climbed up on the bank, but Sam was nowhere to be seen. "Sam, can you hear me," hollered Johnny? There was no response.

What had happened to the life preservers with the money sacks tied to them? Johnny started walking down river along the bank looking for Sam. Around a bend in the river, Johnny spotted Sam sitting on a sandbar. Johnny hollered, "Sam, are you okay?" Sam yelled back, "Yes, but I hit a branch on an underwater log and scraped my side." "I'll go back and get the canoe," said Johnny and he ran back to where the canoe was sticking out of the water. Pulling the canoe up onto the bank, Johnny saw that the scuba tanks were still in it. The hole in the side of the canoe was about the size of Johnny's fist. Johnny took off his pants and cut off one of the legs. Rolling the cut off pant leg into a tight roll, he shoved it into the hole in the canoe. Johnny rolled the canoe on its side and let the water run out. He placed one of the scuba tanks over the hole with the pant leg stuck in it. When Johnny put the canoe back into the river, the patched hole kept the outside water from rushing into the interior.

Johnny had saved one oar and was able to control the canoe down river. He paddled to where Sam was on the sandbar. Johnny told Sam to jump in the canoe. Sam got into the canoe and Johnny said, "We have one oar so I will paddle us to town." "Sam, do you need to go to the emergency room," asked Johnny? "No, it's just a scrape and I need some antibacterial ointment to put on it," said Sam. "Why did you jump out of the canoe," asked Johnny? Sam smiled with one corner of his mouth and said, "To save our treasure." "We don't know where the life preserves are, or if the bags of silver are still tied to them," said Johnny. "We need to get the canoe repaired and then come back and look for the life preservers," said Sam.

Reaching town, the boys dragged the canoe up on to shore. After putting the scuba tanks in the trunk, the boys carried the canoe over to the boat shop for repair. The boat shop owner said he would have it fixed the next day. Then the boys went over to Joe and Evelyn's to get the scuba tanks refilled. "We can go look for the life preservers in a couple of days," said Johnny. We need to move the rest of the coins and look for the other chest," said Sam. "Let's go this Saturday," said Johnny.

The boys picked up the repaired canoe from the boat maker, bought an extra oar and two more life preservers. Then they headed up river, on Saturday morning, to look for the missing life preservers; they rowed up river hoping the bags of silver were still attached to the life preservers. The boys were apprehensive with the thought that someone could have found them by now and could have taken the bags of silver coins. Just below the place where the canoe had struck the underwater log, was a spruce tree, hanging over the river; its expansive lower branches brushed the top of the water. The boys paddled over to the tree and looked underneath the branches. Sure enough, there were the two life preservers caught in the branches. The boys were so relieved to find the orange life preservers. Sam held his breath, as he grabbed one of them. To his utter amazement, the bag of silver coins was still attached. Sam exclaimed, "Hot ziggedy dog,!" Johnny grabbed the other one and was also surprised that it was still attached to the other bag of coins. "Yahoo, mountain dew," hooped Johnny! They both let out a sigh of relief, as they hoisted the bags of silver into the canoe. They tied the life preservers, still attached to the coins, to the canoe; they were afraid that something else, unforeseen, would happen that might cause them to lose their treasure. The boys felt frantic to get back to the safety of their car; they both rowed with a vengeance, as they hurried down river. After carrying the sacks of coins to the car, the boys picked up the canoe and tied it to the top of the car. They felt nervous having this newfound treasure and wanted to hurry back to hide it. They drove back to Sam's farm and hid a sack of coins in the grainery. The other sack of coins Johnny took to his farm and hid it in the straw barn.

Two weeks later, the boys headed up river to get the rest of their treasure. This time, the bags were tied onto the canoe with strong rope and extra knots. It took two trips up river and back, to retrieve the bags of coins they had hidden in the woods. Sam hid half the burlap sacks of coins in the grainery on his farm. Johnny took the remaining sacks of coins and hid them in his straw barn. Now the boys would make an attempt to find the chest full of gold coins, still buried under the silt in Crystal Lake. With scuba tanks full of air, the boys went back to the lake. Using the metal probes to poke through the silt, the boys searched for an hour with no luck. After a short rest, the boys went back into the lake to search some more. They figured the gold weighed more than the silver and would have sunken deeper in the lake. Johnny struck something solid at about three and a half feet into the silt.

I think I found it, thought Johnny, pointing at his probe. Sam swam over and stuck his probe near Johnny's probe. Sam's probe hit the solid object and he gave Johnny a thumbs up. The boys got the paddles and started sweeping away the silt. A much wider area of silt had to be removed, as the object was deeper. After the water had cleared, the boys looked in disbelief at the object in the bottom of the hole. It was another tree that had fallen in the lake at an earlier time. The boys swam back to shore for another rest. "What a lot of work for nothing," grumbled Sam. "We're almost out of air. Let's go back and see if Joe knows where we can rent one of those underwater metal detectors," said Johnny. The boys paddled down river with the tanks and headed for Joe's place. Johnny knocked and Evelyn answered the door. "Hi, boys, come on in," said Evelyn. Sam said, "We need more air for the tanks and wondered if you, or Joe, know where we could rent an underwater metal detector to use." "Joe is not here, but I can fill your tanks with air. We also have an underwater detector that you can borrow. You boys sure are taking this scuba diving in earnest," said Evelyn. "We want to do as much diving as we can before the summer ends," said Johnny. "Next year, we plan to buy our own scuba gear," said Sam. "Are you boys looking for anything special," asked Evelyn? "Just anything we can find," said Sam. "We need the practice using an underwater detector," said Johnny.

The next morning, the boys headed back to the lake with renewed hope. Evelyn had shown the boys how to use the detector and they were excited to start using it. Sam was the first to use it and he got a signal. The boys cleared away the silt and uncovered an old, rusted logging chain. Next, Sam found a piece of tin used for roofing. After finding an old rusted coffee can, the boys went to the shore for their lunch break. "Finding that chest is not as easy as I thought it would be," said Sam. "It might not even be here. Someone may have spotted it a long time ago and retrieved it," said Johnny. "I don't think so, otherwise they would have also seen the chest of silver coins," said Sam. "You're right, Sam, the chest of gold coins is still down there," said Johnny. "You use the detector this time and let's find those gold coins," said Sam with determination. This time, Johnny started searching in deeper water and got a strong signal. He motioned Sam over who stuck his probe through the silt. At about three feet, Sam struck a solid object. The boys cleared the silt away with the paddles. When the water cleared, much to their amazement, they could see the top of a chest. The boys hurried back to shore for the hacksaw and crowbar. Using scuba gear, the boys dove into the water where they had marked the treasure spot. Johnny sawed off the hasp and removed the lock. Sam pried the top of the chest open with the crowbar and it was full of canvas sacks. Johnny reached in and grabbed one of the sacks which split half open, spilling shiny gold coins back into the chest.

Sam and Johnny each grabbed a handful of coins and swam back to shore. Looking at the bright, gold coins in his hand, Johnny said, "Sam, we're rich!" "I can't believe what we have just done," said Sam with a big smile on his face. "The boys couldn't wait and went right back into the water with the pail to get the gold coins. Compared to carrying out the silver coins, a lot less coins could be carried in the pail because gold was heavier than silver. More burlap sacks would be needed for the gold coins. The boys used all the sacks they had and carried the gold to the hollow pine log back in the woods. The remainder of the gold coins would have to be buried in the ground. Sam dug a hole about fifty yards back in the trees, in a small clearing. This would be an easy place to remember, as it was an open spot in the forest about fifty feet across without any trees. Sam paced off the distance to the lake's edge as one hundred sixty three paces; Johnny counted one hundred and sixty seven paces. With the gold coins in the ground, the boys camouflaged their hiding place with tree branches and went back to the lake shore. "Let's load up the canoe and get this gold back home," said Johnny. Sam said, "Johnny, there's something moving in those trees near the edge of the woods." Johnny looked back and saw a mother bear with two cubs. "Let's get out of here. Hurry, let's get to the canoe," yelled Sam!

The boys ran for the canoe, with the mother bear lumbering right behind them. "We can't make it to the canoe in time. Climb a tree," yelled Johnny! The boys climbed up in two separate small oak trees. The bear was on the ground near the trunks of the trees shaking them and trying to climb up. Bears can't climb small trees so the boys were safe for the time being. The bear growled and snorted. It kept trying to push the trees over but they were too strong. The bear stayed around for over an hour trying to get to the boys, but left to go back to her crying cubs.

After the mother bear had left, the boys loaded some of the gold coins into the canoe and headed back to town. When they reached town, they unloaded the sacks of gold coins and carried them to the car. At Sam's farm, the boys carried half the sacks of coins into the grainery. The other half of the gold coins, Johnny took home and hid in the straw barn. It took another trip to bring back all of the coins from the hollow log. "We got all the sacks out of the hollow log, but will still have to make another trip to recover the coins we buried in the clearing," said Johnny." We have about half of the gold coins and all of the silver coins. We have about two hundred fifty pounds, or more, of gold coins," said Sam. Johnny said, "Gold value is at Thirty-two Dollars per ounce and we have at least five hundred pounds of it. We're rich," exclaimed Johnny! "We have at least Two Hundred Twenty Five Thousand Dollars just in gold value. Many of the coins could be worth a lot more depending on the dates and mintmarks. The true value could be, Five Hundred Thousand Dollars or more. "We have enough money for college, to give us a start in our lives and to help out our families," said Johnny. "We can't tell anyone about the coins and just give the money when it is needed," said Sam. "We'll still work all the odd jobs we can to ward off suspicion," said Johnny. "Just remember, Sam, never tell anyone our secret, or everybody and his dog will be hounding us for our money," said Johnny. "I agree", said Sam. "We will take a few coins to several coin dealers to see who gives us the best price. When we find a coin dealer whom we feel we can trust, we will start selling the coins, a few at a time," said Johnny. We will deal in cash and no last names or addresses will be given. I have an uncle who lives in Chicago who wants us to visit him. It would be a perfect opportunity to check on some coin dealers there," said Johnny. "That's a great idea," said Sam.

Johnny told his parents that he had been saving his money and wanted to pay for a trip to Chicago, to visit his uncle. "Are you sure you want to spend your savings to pay for the trip," asked Johnny's father? "Yes," said Johnny. "My college fund is in fine shape." "Okay, we will go," said Johnny's father. Johnny took some silver and gold coins with different dates and mintmarks and put them in a leather pouch.

A few weeks later, they packed the car and drove to Chicago. Chicago is a very large city and there should be many coin dealers there, thought Johnny. After arriving at his uncle's home, Johnny looked up some coin dealers in the yellow pages of the telephone book. There were many coin dealers listed, so Johnny wrote down the addresses of three dealers nearest to his uncle's house according to his map. One dealer was in a shopping mall, so Johnny told his parents that he wanted to take a taxi to the mall to browse. "Be careful," said Johnny's mother. "I'll be okay and won't get lost, as I will be in a taxi cab," said Johnny. He called for a taxi and then went to the mall.

The coin shop was part of a large jewelry store. Johnny went into the jewelry store and walked to a section where the coins were displayed in a large glass case. A man with a mustache and dressed in a suit came to the counter and said, "Can I help you, son?" "Yes," said Johnny. "I have some coins I want you to look at and give me an estimate on their value. Johnny placed the coins on the counter and the man said, "These are some nice coins, where did you get them?" "They were a gift," said Johnny. The man looked in some coin books checking the dates and mint marks. "If you want to sell these coins, I will give you Five Hundred Dollars for them," said the man. "No thanks," said Johnny, as he gathered up the coins and put them back in the leather pouch. Johnny was walking out of the store when the man came running up behind him and said, "I'll give you One Thousand Dollars for those coins." "No thanks," said Johnny and continued walking toward the mall exit and to the taxi stand. Johnny took a taxi to the next coin dealer who offered him Nine Hundred Dollars for the coins then raised it to Fifteen Hundred Dollars. "No thanks," said Johnny. He hailed another cab to go to the third coin dealer's address. The taxi dropped Johnny off at a home that had a sign out front which read, *Antiques and Coins*. The man who answered the door was handicapped with both of his legs missing. He had survived a multiple shark attack while diving for treasure off the coast of Mexico. "I have some coins I want you to look at and give me an estimate of their value," said Johnny. "Okay," said the man whose name was Mickey. "These coins are in excellent condition. Do you want to sell them," asked Mickey? "If the price is right, I will consider selling them," said Johnny. Mickey studied the coins and looked up their value in his books. "One of these coins is worth Three Thousand Dollars," said Mickey. "The total value of the coins you have shown me is Five Thousand Dollars," said Mickey. "I'll pay you eighty percent of the coin value if you want to sell me the coins, young man," said Mickey. "That would be Four Thousand Dollars. I'll take it," said Johnny. "Do you want a check," asked Mickey? "No, thank you, I will take cash," said Johnny. "What is your name, son," asked Mickey? "It's Johnny," replied Johnny. "Johnny, I will have to get your cash out of the safe," said Mickey. Mickey rolled to the back room, got the cash out of the safe and counted it out to Johnny. Then he put it in a brown envelope and handed it to Johnny. "If you have any more coins to sell, please contact me," said Mickey. "I have more coins to sell and will contact you," said Johnny. "With that much cash on you, I will have my wife drive you back to where you're staying," said Mickey. Mickey's wife's name was Phyllis. She was a very pleasant woman, thought Johnny. Johnny had Phyllis drop him off a block from his uncle's house so she wouldn't know the exact address of where he was staying. Johnny thanked her for the ride and stayed on the corner until she was out of sight. This was more money than Johnny had ever had in his hands before and he didn't trust anyone.

When Johnny got back to his uncle's house, his father asked him if he had a good time at the mall. "I had a real good time window shopping," said Johnny. "You're just in time for dinner," said Johnny's Uncle Tom. The diner was excellent and topped off with chocolate pie and vanilla ice cream. Although Johnny was more excited than words could describe, he had to remain calm and with a poker face. He was brimming with excitement but had to be careful not to show it. He had sold five gold and five silver coins for Four Thousand Dollars. He got more money per coin than he could ever have imagined. He couldn't wait to get back and share all this with Sam.

They enjoyed the visit to Chicago and toured many interesting sites. They packed the car, said their goodbyes, and drove back to their farm in the Upper Peninsula of Michigan. The first thing Johnny did when they got home was to rush over to Sam's place with the good news. Johnny handed Sam an envelope with Two Thousand Dollars in it. Sam's eyes opened wide when he looked in the envelope and saw all the money. "Where did you get all this money," asked Sam? "We went to Chicago to visit my uncle. While I was there, I contacted coin dealers to check on the value of our coins. I took five gold and five silver coins with me which I sold for Four Thousand Dollars," said Johnny. "Our coins are worth a fortune," exclaimed Johnny! "Can you trust the coin dealer, asked Sam? "I believe we can. This particular coin dealer will pay in cash with no questions asked. He pays eighty percent of the coin value," said Johnny. "We still have to get the gold coins we buried in the clearing," said Sam. "I have to help my father do some logging, so we might have to wait a few days until I finish," said Johnny.

"How do we sell more coins," asked Sam? "I'll contact the coin dealer in Chicago when we're ready and we'll go and meet him in a town near here; he will bring cash with him," said Johnny. "How do we know if we are getting the right price for the coins," asked Sam? "He will bring us a copy of the current market price on the coins we want to sell," said Johnny. "We will give him the dates and mint marks on each coin so he will know in advance how much money to bring. We will check the price on each coin," said Johnny. "Sounds good to me," said Sam. "You did a terrific job for us while you were in Chicago. I'm so proud to have you for my partner," said Sam. "We will have to keep it a secret between us so that nobody will find out and be asking us for money," said Johnny. "You betcha. I can keep a secret," replied Sam. The boys looked at each other in the eyes, shook hands, and slapped each other's shoulders. At that moment, they bonded for life, in serious friendship.

A few days later, the boys prepared to make a trip to recover the remaining gold coins from the clearing where they were buried. They decided to rent a boat with a motor and pull the canoe behind. The boat maker told Johnny that he could rent the boat but couldn't go up river due to a forest fire. Johnny said he would come back next week instead. Before Johnny could get back to rent the boat, a snowstorm blew in and dropped over a foot of snow with more predicted for the following week. Johnny and Sam decided to wait until the following spring to recover the rest of the gold coins.

After a long, cold winter, spring came and the boys headed up river with a motor boat, pulling the canoe behind. The forest fire had burned all the way to the river and around the lake. There were many more trees down in the stream to the lake. When the boys arrived at the lake, the forest was gone. Where was the clearing with the gold coins the boys wondered? Burned trees were criss-crossed everywhere, including where the clearing had been. The boys searched with the shovel among the downed trees, but couldn't find the clearing with the gold coins. "We will have to search a lot more to find those coins," said Sam. "We need to order a metal detector before we come back and search amongst all these downed, burned trees," said Johnny. "Everything looks different now. However, we know how many paces our hiding place is from the shore," said Sam.

The boys went back down river, disappointed at not finding the gold coins. They went to Joe's and asked for an address to order a metal detector. Joe said, "You can use my underwater detector." "No thanks. We want a detector of our own instead of always borrowing one," said Sam. "I understand," said Joe and he gave the boys a telephone number and an address, to a reputable metal detector manufacturing company, in Detroit. The boys left Joe's house and called the number that he had given them. The cost of the detector was One Hundred Ninety Dollars plus shipping and handling cost of Five Dollars. The boys got a money order for the correct amount and mailed it that same day. They were told it would take a week to receive the detector. "We have a lot of money right now, and we have plenty of time to look for our lost gold coins," replied Johnny. "You're right, Johnny. Let's take it easy for a while and enjoy our new found wealth; we have all summer to find those coins," said Sam. Johnny had received a letter from Sandy saying that she would be spending the summer with her aunt and uncle on their farm. She said she couldn't wait to see him. This was going to be a great summer, thought Johnny.

Would you like to see your manuscript become a book?

If you are interested in becoming a PublishAmerica author, please submit your manuscript for possible publication to us at:

mybook@publishamerica.com

You may also mail in your manuscript to:

**PublishAmerica
PO Box 151
Frederick, MD 21705**

www.publishamerica.com